CIRCUS GIRL

A NOVEL

ELIZABETH CARTER WELLINGTON

ARCHWAY
PUBLISHING

This book is a work of fiction. Any references to historical events, real
people, or real places are used fictitiously. Other names, characters, places,
and events are products of the author's imagination, and any resemblance to
actual events or places or persons, living or dead, is entirely coincidental.

Archway Publishing books may be ordered
through booksellers or by contacting:

Archway Publishing
1663 Liberty Drive
Bloomington, IN 47403
www.archwaypublishing.com
1 (888) 242-5904

Because of the dynamic nature of the Internet, any web addresses or
links contained in this book may have changed since publication and
may no longer be valid. The views expressed in this work are solely those
of the author and do not necessarily reflect the views of the publisher,
and the publisher hereby disclaims any responsibility for them.

Cover photograph provided by author.

ISBN: 978-1-4808-3470-5 (sc)
ISBN: 978-1-4808-3468-2 (hc)
ISBN: 978-1-4808-3469-9 (e)

Library of Congress Control Number: 2016913971

Scripture quotations are taken from the King James Version.

Print information available on the last page.

Archway Publishing rev. date: 9/27/2016

CONTENTS

For Edward "Red" Maynard,
canvas boss, storyteller
In Memoriam

MOTH YEARS

1

never thought of myself as Sarah Cunningham, the teenage runaway. I used to tell people that I walked away with the circus. Today I barely recognize the person I was at seventeen—a headstrong girl consumed by wanderlust, confused by passionate feelings that seemed to come out of nowhere. I was a singing arrow without a target.

Maybe I took to the road that summer because all my friends were away, including my boyfriend, who was traveling in Malaysia. Almost all the senior guys in the art crowd at high school—the "freaks"—had decided to go overland to South Asia after graduation.

It was 1971. Young backpackers bought *Europe on 5 Dollars a Day*, crossed the Atlantic, and kept on going. No one had written *The Guide to Hitching Rides on Tops of Trucks in Afghanistan* or *How to Get Hash in Nepal*. My generation would create those travel guides for themselves. They would share information, their survival stories at youth hostels and fleabag rooms all across the Third World, congregating at places like Goa and Kathmandu.

Although I was the competitive type, a fault that came from growing up in the Boston "W" suburbs, I had to content myself with finding amusement and adventure in more conventional ways that summer.

I can remember calling up Big Al, the only guy left in town from my boyfriend's circle of friends, to see about going to the Hatch Shell for the Boston fireworks on the Fourth of July. Even as we stretched out on a picnic blanket as the music played, we remained side by side, burning to be held but staying in our respective lanes as friends. He would later become a movie director in Israel.

It was like that then. We were all hell-bent on being extraordinary. Most of our families didn't know what to do with us. We had all read *The Politics of Experience* by R.D. Laing and shared an enthusiasm for pot, Jorge Luis Borges, The Who (my boyfriend), and The Incredible String Band (me).

Meanwhile, back in the world of grownups, Dad came home after work and lay down on the sofa after a pass at the liquor cabinet; he remained prone until dinner, fully dressed in business attire except for removing his jacket and tie. Mom got dinner together, an effort that was lost on her gaggle of ripening teenagers. We barely sat through a meal without exploding into laughter, and we disappeared into our rooms within minutes after arriving at the table. It was a time when restlessness was everywhere. And I was the wildest one of the bunch, always climbing trees and lurking in the combat zone on the backstreets of Chinatown late at night with my boyfriend. I was just curious about sex, about real life. I would tell lies to get a crack at a raw experience that would mark me forever. I had been to lots of foreign films at the Orson Welles Cinema in Central Square. I knew there were lives to be had that were nothing like mine.

My traditional WASP name—Sarah Cunningham—had recently been entered in the *Boston Social Register,* and in the fall, I would begin receiving invitations on creamy velum to tea dances so that I could meet the "right people." But I yearned to abandon this script and asked to have my name removed. No, there would be no coming-out party for me as a Boston *Mayflower* debutante.

But to be honest, I was still very much at loose ends and resentful of any parental intrusion on my private ruminations about the future. That June, I had graduated from high school a year early without making plans to go to college.

"Well, what *do* you want to do?" my father would ask, to which I would respond hotly, "I don't *know!* But I'm not going to sit around and *rot.*" I could only define myself in terms of what I didn't want, like a murky figure emerging from the blank space of a photo negative.

Having tried and failed at a summer waitressing job, I convinced my parents to let me take a short summer course in film and photography at an experimental school in the Berkshires. For a week in July, I could get the hell out of my suburban hometown where nothing—I mean, *nothing*—was happening.

Photography seemed to suit me perfectly. I liked hunting and trapping images of a time that was passing. My friends and I could all sense it—the shifting of the centuries. All the remnants of the Industrial Revolution were being knocked down, thrown out, or dismantled.

The previous winter, when I got my learner's permit, I practiced driving the family station wagon; it was a giant blue Cutlass with power everything that handled like a ship. I wasn't much of a driver. I'd slam on the brakes at an intersection and stare in bewildered confusion at the street signs in downtown Boston. Every street corner looked the same to me, and I got lost—often. My heart would still be beating fast when I managed to shimmy the overpowered vehicle through to the next block. On weekends, I let my older friends take turns at the wheel so that we could drive from the suburbs into the South End where our high school art teacher rented a vast open space in an old warehouse.

Sometimes my boyfriend, Big Al, and I would spend a January afternoon wandering through the graveyard of warehouses and shops, rescuing pieces of old Americana. Big Al would take pictures. In a long winter coat and funky felt hat, I can remember striking a pose in the blasted-out shell of a shop window, glass crunching under my boots.

It took three of us, all fellow art students, to shoulder a twelve-foot wooden sign and carry it up the pitched stairs to our teacher's loft. The sign was black with raised wooden letters; once painted gold, it had faded to the color of driftwood.

Wood was replaced by steel, warm surfaces and textures traded for hard, cold ones. It was the end of the small coffee shops with yellowed newspapers and regulars who had time to talk. We foresaw the end of village life in the city, but we scrambled to keep bits of it alive by learning to make things with our own hands and writing long letters illustrated with elaborately penned drawings. We planted food, learned to bake bread, and cooked Third World dishes. Our little circle of high school art and theater friends even made hummus from scratch. My boyfriend, Big Al, and the others would sit with their legs outstretched on the linoleum kitchen floor, peeling the skin off each chickpea while swapping stories for movie plots.

Every day another piece of the past was missing until it finally became clear that the only way to turn back the clock was to climb on a plane and make tracks for the Old World, then the Ancient World, and then the Third World. We took it upon ourselves to reclaim what was lost. But at the time, we were barely able to embrace the madness of adolescence.

My boyfriend began the journeying phase by hopping freight cars, getting as far from Boston as Canada. He traveled with Big Al, and like a pair of hobos, they curled up to sleep in fetal positions in boxcars. If we could not recover the early twentieth century, then at least we could star ourselves in our own imaginary movie about it.

★ ★ ★

So there it was, staring me in the face: a colorful vintage poster of an opened-mouthed tiger stapled to a phone pole. A circus had come to the little college town in the Berkshires where I was learning how to count out minutes and seconds in the darkroom in the gloom of a red light.

My experiences at the photography course during the first few days had been somewhat mundane. For lack of good live subjects, I had photographed old beat-up suitcases filled with folkloric clothing, mirrored Indian shawls, and unfamiliar hats. My classmates behaved like chattering monkeys high up in their intellectual trees—highly verbal suburban kids from New York and Boston, like me. The boys especially were all vying madly to make the ultimate pithy statement, but I guessed that sex was on their minds. I felt it too, like a current of longing continually shifting the ground beneath my feet, begging me to break down and surrender.

I became quiet—a female-going-underground kind of quiet; a certain wildness radiated from my body, attracting young men in a steady stream. But at night, after hours of dancing a sweaty bump-and-grind with students who were much older, I found myself closing my dorm room door on the last guy to follow me to my room, even as he protested, "Aw, come on, Sarah, honey. Now I'm going to have to beat the meat."

You see, I have a boyfriend. But all I really had was his picture and an aerogram or two. I used to race to the end of the aerograms, without reading them, to see if he had signed off with *love*. For all the skinny-dipping and rolling around with boys I'd done, I was still a virgin, although barely. And that was only because I managed to keep my jeans on. Every teenage girl I knew had lots of practice with "other ways" to satisfy the guys, and I was no different. Being too young to get a prescription for the pill didn't stop me. One time I pitched my tent in a pasture and fooled around with a couple of guys at once, knowing they'd be too embarrassed to take things very far. Guys would pressure me when I held back. Older girls had the pill, so what was my excuse if I was sexually curious? And I had to agree, it felt so damn good. Jesus! As my boyfriend used to say, "The rush is better than heroin."

But my excuse was always the same. I wanted to go all the way with my boyfriend when he returned. I didn't want to give it up to just anybody. In his absence, I finally managed to convince my doctor to fit me for a diaphragm. I was ready.

The end of my correspondence to "Boyfriend, c/o Poste Restante" came when he wrote to let me know how heavy her hair was when he held it in his hand, a shining black curtain that fell in lustrous sheets when she moved off of him. I guess that was in Penang, and he had found what he was looking for. Not to be outdone, I took my camera and got a ride to the circus.

★ ★ ★

Once I reached the grassy lot, I immediately began taking black-and-white photographs. A Spanish girl sporting a henna-red pony tail and spit curls crouched on the metal steps attached to her camper with her chin in her hands. She was watching three young acrobats—one boy and two girls—as they practiced their tumbling in leotards and tights. She smiled at them, showing her large white teeth, which were perfect except for one gold incisor tooth. The door of another camper opened, and an Indian man in a jeweled turban stepped out into the sunlight. He was carrying his lovely infant daughter—an exquisite child with mild, angelic features that served as a foil for the fierce intelligence in her eyes. When she caught sight of me, I was unnerved by the intensity of her gaze; two dark eyes came at me like black darts. I could barely make out the mother in the shadows behind her husband. I wavered and lowered my camera. Stepping lightly with long, tan legs, she emerged from her trailer like a butterfly breaking out of its cocoon. She was a beauty from the Philippines with delicate features, expressive eyebrows, and shiny black hair that fell to her waist.

The Indian man looked at me with the direct gaze that all circus people seemed to share. With a theatrical sweeping gesture, he said, "Gentle lady, I see that you are on a quest for something that has yet to appear."

"I'm looking for good things to photograph ... do you mind?" I held the Nikon to my face and adjusted the lens. "I'm Sarah." Click. Click. "And I'm not a lady, exactly," I added with a short laugh.

"And I am known as Billy Gunga, the circus conjurer and magician. It appears that I have been chosen to reveal the circus to you." The powerfully attractive, dark-skinned man gave a reverential bow and extended his arm toward the canvas tent. "Enter through the curtains of the big top, Lady Sarah."

Shouldering my camera strap, I walked down the midway, past the cotton candy and soda machines and a little wooden shack where toy circus animals hung like ornaments from lines strung across a propped-open window. At the entrance to the big top, there were heavy velvet curtains hanging under a large banner that read "Sideshow" in red and gold letters. A very old, white-haired man, who introduced himself as Red, sat in a folding chair at the entrance, ready to take tickets. I asked him if I could take pictures of the performers under the big top while they rehearsed.

"Sure, go on ahead. We won't be open for a couple of hours." He waved his hand and let me pass through without paying. "The elephants are practicing their tricks. Tell West; he's working the bulls right now."

"Bulls? What about the elephants?" I cocked my head, confused.

"Hah! You must be a farm girl!" The old man was clearly delighted. "Bulls is what we call elephants in the circus. Male, female, don't matter which. Now go on in and find West; tell him Red sent you!" he called out after me.

Once inside, there was so much for me to take in. The tent was large, easily covering the distance of a football field. On the grassy ground, three large wooden rings—painted in red-and-white stripes—were set up for different acts. Two female performers, twins with blond ponytails, brushed past me wearing outfits that revealed more butt cheek and cleavage than I had ever seen on the street. Awkwardly, I tied up the ends of my blouse to show a bit of midriff, creating a Gypsy Rose Lee effect.

Then I saw him—a slender young man with long dark hair, dressed in the faded red coverall jumpsuit worn by all the Reyes Bros. Ragtime Gypsy Show roustabouts. I picked up my camera and took a quick shot from a distance. The camera caught the circus boy as he was raising his hand over his head to command one of the elephants. "Up, Bessie! Up!" he bellowed.

The female elephant slowly reared up in a deliberate fashion and sat on a painted circus drum, her front legs in the air, trunk raised in an appealing tea-cup-handle loop. Later, in the dark room as I developed this photograph, I would be convinced that the elephant was smiling.

A second elephant became aware of my approach before her handler did. She ambled over to me, flapping her ears and snorting up clouds of sawdust with her trunk. Perhaps she thought my camera was something to eat. I quickly shifted my strap so that the camera hung down my back.

"Mary! What're you doing there, Mary?" West called after the beast as she stepped out of the ring and made her way toward me at a trot. Some of the other performers who were practicing laughed and called out to the young elephant handler, "Better keep your bulls in line there, West!"

In the center ring, a stout, sandy-haired man with thick muscular legs was not amused. He stood in an attitude of tense disapproval while a dark-haired female performer snaked her legs around the two ropes suspending her static trapeze bar and hung upside down. The heavyset man kept his eyes on the aerialist dangling in the air over his head, but his face was grim. "You shouldn't let your elephant run loose in the ring," he growled at West in a thick Nordic accent. "For this, we have the electric cattle prod, no?"

"Don't worry, Swede; I can handle her without a hot shot!" West raced at a full run to catch up with his wayward elephant and commanded in a booming voice, "Mary, come!"

As soon as the elephant turned around to face her handler, he bounded up her trunk, gripped her head harness, and landed himself gracefully behind her ears in position to ride her back to the ring. I realized he had already seen me when he looked back at me over his shoulder and said, "Sorry about this, ma'am. Mary doesn't mean any harm; she's just curious."

"Thank goodness! I was scared for a minute there." I let out a breath and moved no farther.

All at once, the young man jumped off the elephant's back, slid easily to the ground, and led the elephant over to me. "Want a ride? I'm West, by the way." The circus boy looked right at me with a cat-like stare.

"I'm … uh … Sarah." His sudden approach, the dazzling quality of his smile—all of it made it almost impossible for me to speak. Collecting myself, I added, "Sarah Cunningham" and then felt foolish for making a proper introduction. I lowered my eyes, slipped the camera strap off my shoulder, and set my Nikon down on the ring curb. As if I had already answered, West put his hands on my waist and lifted me onto Mary's trunk. I climbed up the short hill of her brow, turned, and settled on her broad neck as West followed, hopping lightly into place behind me. The circus boy dug in his heels and urged the elephant forward. I noticed he wasn't carrying a stick or anything else that could be used as a crop; he commanded the elephant with nothing more than his voice, legs, and feet. His arms were wrapped around my waist, holding me steady with a subtle pressure that left its meaning ambiguous. The enigmatic feeling would stay with me for days after I left the big top and the Berkshires and headed back home.

"It must be fun to perform in the circus," I said, feeling the lurch of the large animal moving beneath us. The circus boy's folded hands rested lightly on the exposed skin of my midriff.

For a brief moment, I felt like I belonged there—that I had been magically transformed into a showgirl who beamed and waved at the crowd in a feathered headdress and sequined brassiere.

West called out to a petite Hispanic woman in costume who had joined the other performers—two clowns—in the far ring with the other elephant. "Hey, Serpentina, I'm coming!"

I felt like a tourist again when I was helped to the ground by the clown men. Introductions were made all around. I greeted each person and then took candid shots of their well-worn faces without makeup, so different from their performance personae. In the ring, the clowns' expressions changed with fluidity from tragic to whimsical. White pancake usually erased the busy map of expression lines I could see clearly through the lens.

The diminutive Cuban performer introduced herself to me, a townie, with her stage name, "I'm known as Serpentina in the sideshow," she said as she positioned herself next to West so that I could get a shot of the two of them in front of an elephant. She was a peppy woman with a heavy Spanish accent who wore her hair piled in a high bouffant on her head like a beauty queen. The Indian elephant could lift up Serpentina's small body with her trunk and place her on her back to ride in one go.

"I'm the snake lady who gets the knives put through her in a box, you know?" The Cuban performer smiled wide for the camera, lipstick glowing.

"Sure, I used to ask to see the woman in the box all the time when I was kid," I grinned at her. "But they would only let the men go up to look. And there was always a long line."

Serpentina laughed heartily from the chest, "I know … is good trick."

As I exited the big top, I ran into the old man, Red, again. He motioned to me to take a seat next to him on a hay bale and keep him company for a while. I looked up at the billboard-sized paintings of a fire eater, a sword swallower, and a snake charmer that lined the midway.

"You got all these acts in the sideshow?" I asked.

"That's nothing," scoffed Red. "In the old days, they used to show a woman's corpse pickled in formaldehyde!"

"No kidding?"

I snapped a few pictures of the colorful murals painted with childlike simplicity on the sides of the circus trucks. When I directed the lens at Red's jagged, wrinkled face, he asked, "You see West?"

"Yeah. Is he from a circus family?" I asked.

"Ha!" Red gave a shout of laughter. "Not likely, unless he was adopted by a family of chimpanzees. Tarzan is what I call him!" He shifted his weight toward me, leaned his elbow on one knee, and launched into a story. "I'll never forget the day that skinny boy joined the show in Florida. There was something strange about him. Hardly made a sound, always keeping an eye out while he ate, like an animal. When I'd say, 'Where you from, boy?' he'd just look at me with them beady animal eyes and say, 'I been living in the swamp.'" Red cackled, threw back his head, and slapped his thigh.

The tent flaps parted, and West appeared. He had changed out of his coveralls into a pair of rumpled Levi's and a striped T-shirt that was open at the chest. His skin was shining with perspiration. The circus boy smiled broadly at Red, but he remained very still, listening intently.

Red didn't seem to notice West's shadow at all, and he leaned forward, as if to let me in on a secret. "I asked him, 'What's the matter, boy, you running?' Soon as I asked, he stopped eating and looked around to see if it was time to go. He said he wanted to work with the animals and make them do tricks and such. I figured he had the know-how from living so long in the wild. But as a new circus hand—a first of May, we call 'em—'bout the closest he got to the animals was right behind 'em, with a shovel!" The old man let out a raspy laugh, leaning over all the way, bending at the waist, and pushing at my knee to make me smile.

"So he's not a performer?" I chanced a quick look at West. He was listening in a relaxed attitude, one arm draped over the hood of the office truck. He seemed to be looking with interest at the embroidered moon and stars I'd sewn along the hem of my bell-bottomed pants.

"A kinker? Hell no. West is no performer, just an animal handler. And he takes care of the whole menagerie. But, you know, that boy ought to be performing instead of that big load of nothing—," he intoned using an announcer's vibrato, "—Humberto the Magnificent!" Red waved his hand theatrically in the air. "I see him sitting up in his trailer all day, playing cards, and powdering his nose. That bull man is supposed to be a star, but he never comes down to the ring between shows to practice routines with the elephants. He lets this boy here, his menagerie boy, do it for him." Red jerked his head in West's direction. "And to tell you the truth, half the time, West does more than just move the props around during the elephant act. Mary and Bessie listen to him. I've seen it with my own eyes."

West smiled to himself. Then he slipped off his T-shirt, hung it on the rearview mirror, and sat down with his bare back propped up against a truck tire, arms resting on his knees. He looked away from me, his eyes directed at someone I couldn't see. I lifted my camera and took the shot.

So the circus boy had a story, I thought. He had wandered onto the circus grounds and stayed long enough to become one of them; he was a wild one, like me.

When it was time to leave for the college campus, I said my good-byes and promised everyone I would come back and give them their photographs at their next stop. West appeared at my side and offered to walk me to the edge of the grounds where my ride was waiting.

I don't remember if we talked much or what we said. He was quiet in a way that stripped all conversation down to the essentials. I only have one entry in my diary about that first encounter with West: "I want to go to South America with you, get some animals, and you can take pictures," he'd said. What I do remember is that a shock of dark hair fell into his light brown eyes, and he didn't bother sweeping it back. He was twenty.

He reminded me of the farm hands I'd met on my grandmother's farm in New Hampshire, the ones who loaded hay bales in the sun. Their torsos glowed, and they all had watery pale lines just visible above their belts as they stretched and hurled the bales up onto the hay truck. Maybe, like them, this circus boy had gotten tired of throwing bales all day and even more tired of taking farmers' daughters out to the drive-in on Saturday nights.

Finally, we stopped at the edge of the lot and faced each other. Leaning over slightly, he pulled a blue file card out of his back pocket and handed it to me. The route card. He pronounced *route* as "rowt" instead of "root."

"If you want to come back, follow the route card," he said simply. I received the card like a talisman and stared at the list of dates: two weeks' worth of engagements in tiny towns, with the mileage for each morning's haul listed in the final column.

"Look for the red arrows on the phone poles once you get into town to guide you to the lot. One arrow means keep going straight. Two arrows means turn here. Three arrows means you've arrived." When West looked directly into my eyes this time, his expression was gentle, unguarded.

The Reyes Bros. Ragtime Gypsy Show was headed south, always south, until it reached winter quarters in Florida. I promised to return. "I'll wait for you." He gave me a smile—a brief, enigmatic flash—and then he disappeared behind the maze of trucks and canvas.

★ ★ ★

When I found myself back in the dark room, I held my breath as chemicals washed over damp paper. There he was, sitting bare-chested against the tread of an enormous truck tire, light playing on the smooth skin of his shoulders, the magnificent excitement of his muscular forearms at rest, the beautiful neck and high cheekbones illuminated, and the amber-colored feline eyes looking away.

For our final project in the photography class, we were asked to choose our best shot to turn into a photo silkscreen. I wasn't sure what high contrast would do to the cherished picture of my circus boy, but the dark, seductive elements in the image exploded off the wet paper. The striped T-shirt, hung up to dry, leaped out in black and white in the foreground. The thick truck tires gave an illusion of permanence. The face, the throat, and the bare chest of the boy seemed to reveal a sensuality that I had only glimpsed through his peculiar cat-like movements at the big top. West's eyes watched furiously, missing nothing. I hadn't noticed the intensity of his expression before. Reduced to black and white, his face was clearly readable. I could tell that running was in his blood the way it was in mine. I sensed in him a terrible urge to rush at life, pierce its skin, and damn the consequences.

I approached the photography instructor, hopelessly gushing. "Isn't he beautiful?"

The woman with dark-framed glasses and wiry salt-and-pepper hair poised herself at the edge of the well but did not dive in. "Yes," she said and added pointedly, "it's a beautiful image."

I let it pass. Falling in was so much more delicious than hanging at the water's edge. But that is when my female silences began, at moments when I sensed the tacit disapproval from others of everything that surged with excitement. Adults were somewhere else, going to prescribed destinations—to the bank, the golf course, the supermarket. I was determined to create a different path. I would reinvent my landscape and become a traveling gypsy.

Back then, people talked about the generation gap. The post-war baby boom created a groundswell of teenage rebellion.

Grownups grumbled about the impetuous folly of youth—all that long hair, hitchhiking and free love. Many of us were on a terrifying course beyond the garden gate. But most parents were certain that their children would at least give a backward glance before leaving and remember to return home to safety just in time. I was not one of those children. I was filled with a kind of blind emotion—part will, part anxiety, part lust—a drive I can hardly explain. The urge was something beyond curiosity; it was an unbridled rush to know, to experience, to feel, like a moth circling a flame, around and around, fascinated by the fire, willing to approach the light and singe its wings. When I think back on that time—the circling, the blindness, the heart out of control—I have my own private title for it: "The Moth Years."

LEAVING HOME

2

he summer photography course came to an end. I packed my portfolio of mounted black-and-white circus photographs and took them to my grandmother's farm in Rock Mountain, New Hampshire, population 114. The locals, mostly seniors and farming families, took a dim view of my siblings and me when we came for the summer; they called us "the hippies on the hill."

Heading to my grandmother's farm for the summer was an annual family ritual. Once the academic year ended at our exclusive schools in the Boston suburbs, my mother would bring her brood up to the farm to let us loose. We would leave Massachusetts in June for the rural backwater where my mother was born. She kept us in New Hampshire the entire summer, away from crowds; polio was still a concern. The vaccine only arrived on the scene when I was in fourth grade. It was distributed at school in the gymnasium: a sugar cube with a violet-colored dot of medicine that stained the white sugar.

In the country, I naturally learned to care for animals—wild and domestic—alongside the sons and daughters of farming families. I could run down the top of a stone wall without losing my balance, nurse an injured crow back to health, milk a cow by hand, ride a pony bareback, and recognize bear spoor.

To trap a loose hog in a barn, I was taught to grab a deep rubber feed bucket and plunge the hog's head in, snout first, and hold it over its face like a mask until it couldn't see. Then, still holding the bucket tightly, I had to coil its pigtail around my free hand like a rope and steer the animal back to its pen, squealing and skittering all the way.

My three brothers and I spent a lot of time with the cows, mostly because we enjoyed exploring and wandering through the open pastures. My favorite words of high summer were, "The cows are out!" That exclamation led to my favorite kind of chaos. I would run outside barefoot, and, in my pajamas, join the band of family members who had gathered to form a human corral. With arms spread wide, we'd herd the cattle toward the field where they'd broken through. The yelling, the pandemonium, and the thrill of upending the evening ritual of brushed teeth, stories, and the Lord's Prayer lit me up like a firework. I wanted to live that way forever.

But that summer, childhood delights were somehow being replaced by unfamiliar impulses, a strange emotional blend of hurt, anger, and pleasure. Now that I was a teenager, the farm held no excitement for me.

I passed the long, lonely days in a daydream, sewing. Rummaging through the attic for material, I discovered an old trunk of Victorian clothing and proceeded to design costumes to wear at the circus by adding embroidered Indian fabric borders to the hems of petticoats and linen knickers. I even went so far as to sew small mirrors from Rajasthan into a red-and-yellow striped vest.

During the day, I helped paint the barn and care for the goat and chickens in worn out men's hand-me-downs that fit like prison clothes. The shapeless overalls piled around my ankles, and the pant hem was pungent with the smell of manure. My brothers worked for a neighboring dairy farmer and got to spend their days outside, shirtless. I envied them. At night, I retreated to my bedroom, pulled out the route card, and studied a map of Pennsylvania that I'd picked up at the general store, the only shop in town.

My boyfriend had stopped writing to me—still smoking hash all day in Penang with that dark-haired woman in his bed, I imagined. Most of my friends were in Boston or traveling the world, the way I wished I could. I threw away the photo my boyfriend had sent me before he'd reached Malaysia, taken by a street photographer in Delhi. Somehow, he was made to have a shiny, round face, like a male star in a Bollywood movie—with dark eyes, arched eyebrows, and pink skin. He became unreal to me. I confided in my mother about my boyfriend; at least part of what I told her was true. She was always sympathetic in matters of the broken heart.

"Sometimes I think the first love is the only real love of your life," she said. "When my first real boyfriend told me we should end it, I went home and threw up."

"Why did you end it then?" I asked.

We were weeding the vegetable garden, which made it easier to talk. We didn't have to look each other in the eye, and our emotions could flow through our bodies and into our hands. Pulling up weeds by the roots felt good, like extracting thorns from wounded places inside.

"I wasn't the one who ended it," she said softly.

"That must have been horrible." I glanced up at her. A mane of shoulder-length chestnut curls was held back from her forehead by a knotted red bandana as she bent over her work.

"It was very hard. During wartime, you know, it's such an unnatural way to live—all the women here and all the eligible men there, fighting a war. We were all waiting, writing letters to men some of us didn't even know to keep up their spirits. My first love called it off before he shipped out. He didn't want me to pine away for him or put my life on hold in case he never came back."

"Did he? Did he come back?"

"He did, but by then, I had a new beau and a big diamond on my finger."

"Dad, right?" I smiled and looked at her sideways.

"I flaunted my fiancé in his face. See what I've got now?" My mother never stopped digging up roots and working the soil as she spoke. Her movements were rhythmic, her hands full of experience.

"You got back at him for dumping you. Wow." I sat back on my heels and rested for a moment, watching my mother as she picked up a trowel and chipped into the dirt, digging a hole to bury the dead chipmunk the cat had left on the doormat by the kitchen door that morning.

"It doesn't mean that I never cared for him. Sometimes I wonder what would have happened if I'd waited. Your father just came in and swept me off my feet with his manners, and his Boston Brahmin family was so much wealthier than ours. It was a different world."

"I don't want to wait for *any* man. They can fry for all I care!"

My mother laughed with abandon, a lilting ripple of sound that danced like sunlight on water. "Good for you," she said, patting the loose dirt down with the back of the trowel blade.

At dinner at my grandmother's house that night, I eyed everyone at the table as if I had arrived from an alien planet. There we were, as a family, sitting around the old oak table, picking up forks, and listening to ice crack and tinkle in the glasses. The peaceful domesticity of the farmhouse suddenly became odious. When I retreated to my room upstairs, my sense of alienation became acute. I glared at the neatly-made beds with their perfect hospital corners and folded quilts.

This buttoned-down life would end for me soon. Now that I knew there was an escape from it all, a place where I could ride an elephant into the river, I was ready to move on. I wanted to put my feet up on the dashboard in the cab of a semitruck while the circus boy drove, glancing at me sideways and sliding his fingers into mine. I wanted it so much.

Something very alive and dangerous was prowling inside me, and I let go of all caution, utterly defenseless against an onslaught of fantasies of life on the road with West. Hot days, dog days were slipping by, and I couldn't help but think about the circus and the circus people on the long mornings by myself, up on a ladder, painting the barn. I was being carried off like a leaf sucked along by a current.

On one of my last nights at the farmhouse, I called our collie from his spot on the porch and made my way through the pastures below. The grass was so tall I could hardly make out the collie navigating through the familiar path; flashes of golden fur were all I saw of him. I was careful not to trample the hay crop, and I followed the stone wall until the house was lost from view. I walked until I reached the edge, where the forest became dark and dense, and I stripped and began to run naked, breasts and heels flying, the dog barking and jumping beside me. The fading sun on that sultry summer evening reached out fingers of orange light through the trees. Warm breezes played at my face and along my bared arms. I wanted to embrace something powerful, magical, and transporting—to lose myself somehow.

I had made my decision: I was in love with the circus boy, and I would follow the route card until I reached him. I took shelter in the trees and put my clothes back on, suddenly embarrassed by my naked romp in the field. An understanding grasped at me. My days of finding rapture in fantasy were at an end. If I wanted to feel, really feel something, I would have to give myself to the young man who had found me by placing his hands on my waist and inviting me to run away with the circus. Back in my room with the door closed, I sat on the bedroom floor with my maps out. There, I plotted my route and packed my circus clothes in an army duffel. The places and dates on the route card had hovered at the edges of my mind for days. Bloomsburg, Pennsylvania. July twenty-third.

I propped open a diamond-shaped window to breathe in the smell of an approaching thunderstorm. In the distance, a strange violet light was lifting off the mountains. Something about the timeless way night fell on that summer evening filled me with a rare nostalgia, and it made me join the circus at the age of seventeen, with no driver's license and no summer job. Just a camera and a route card.

★ ★ ★

The bus reached Bloomsburg at twilight. I sat up front next to the bus driver, alert to the red arrows on the telephone poles, trying to make out where the circus had set up in the town. I was the last person left on board. The bus driver was kind and steered his way through back streets, picking up the trail, watching for circus spotlights. When it grew too dark to spot circus posters or red arrows, we finally asked some people walking in the street—circus-goers who carried toy whips and hula hoops—and we were directed to a vast lot behind a Woolco.

"Well, here you are," the driver said, lowering his head to have a good look out the door into the semi-darkness. He let me out by a phone booth; my guess was that he hoped I'd call my parents to tell them I'd made it safely.

The telephone booth was occupied. A pale man in his twenties—an almost albino blond—stood with his back to me. He was wearing frayed cutoffs and a muscle shirt, but he had no muscles or tattoos on his arms to go with it. He was thin and flaccid, like an overcooked noodle. I thought I heard him say, "This is Superman," and I had to stifle a laugh. The pale man closed the phone booth door as soon as he saw me approach, leaned into the receiver, and cupped his mouth. I didn't have to wait long.

"All yours," said the young man with a tepid smile as he exited smoothly and headed toward the circus grounds. I dropped a dime into the pay phone and called collect, reversing the charges. It was dark out, after nine o'clock, but the air was still warm. I kept the door of the dusty phone booth open.

"Hi, Mom."

"Is that you, Sarah? Is everything okay?"

"Yeah, Mom. I'm fine," I said. There was a short pause before my mother filled the silence.

"You found the circus?"

"Yeah, I made it!" I said a bit too enthusiastically. "The bus driver was really nice," I added to reassure her.

"Where are you?"

"Right now I'm outside a restaurant. The circus people bought me dinner," I lied—already beginning to weave the story I would fabricate to please her.

"I'm glad they're taking good care of you."

"Oh sure. I think the acrobats and aerialists really liked their photographs." I knew how to capture my mother's imagination. I was feeding her material for the stories she could tell her friends.

"So, you're going to Altoona next?"

"Yeah, Mom. Don't worry, okay? You have a copy of our route card. Wherever it says is where I'll be. I'm with the circus now." Those words filled me with such satisfaction: *I'm with the circus now.*

"I'm proud of you, Sarah," my mother said in her warmest voice.

"Thanks, Mom."

At the time, I didn't realize I was being handled. Later, my mother told me she used words of praise to flatter me, hoping to extend the conversation with her self-centered adolescent. It was the only way she felt she could maintain contact with me. Her daughter was quickly slipping away from everything she had ever known.

"Sarah? Sweetheart?"

"What?" I was anxious to end the call and make contact with the circus people before they turned in for the night.

"We're going on vacation in a couple of weeks, remember? Your father and the boys are going out West to the ranch in Jackson Hole."

I waited. There was a charged silence.

"You know we'd love to have you join us if you want to come along," she said.

Our conversation immediately became stilted, its initial intimacy hampered by the careful courtesy we used in our family to bridge moments of tension—starchy expressions like "be that as it may," "as far as I'm concerned," or one-word placeholders that meant nothing, like "indeed."

"I don't know," I said, playing for time. "Why don't I give you a call next week? I may be under contract to stay with the show until the end." At seventeen, I liked the word *contract*. It sounded so important—my first real summer job. Making one's own money was the key to attaining status in my family. Our conversation ended with an agreement that I'd place collect calls on my days off, which, according to the route card, would most likely be on Sunday layovers.

Shouldering my duffel bag, I headed toward the wide blue-and-white stripes of the tent wall, weaving my way through a corridor of stakes and yellow guy lines. The smell of diesel, popcorn, and sticky sweet cotton candy syrup was familiar. The circus boy's voice could be heard coaxing Bessie forward. "Move up, Bessie. Move up!" A portion of the big top collapsed as the main pole was pulled from its upright position by the elephant. I'd arrived at teardown.

CIRCUS MARRIAGE

3

I ducked under a yellow guy line and headed for a section where the lights were still set up in the midway. The scene was eerie now that the people had gone. The grandstand where Serpentina performed was empty; only her trick box remained, bristling with the seven swords that would perforate her body twice a day. Two strings of bare bulbs swung back and forth in the warm night, throwing light on the ghoulish faces painted on the circus trucks behind the grandstand. Each painted circus tableau was rendered in primitive fashion: a clown, a snake charmer, a fire eater.

This was the three-ring traveling circus I had seen as a child every summer in New Hampshire, the kind of show that asked the men in the crowd for a "silver donation" (a dime or a quarter would do) to see what the half-naked lady looked like all contorted inside her box with the swords run through. The rednecks would press forward to climb the short set of stairs to the sideshow grandstand to look in. Some stared into the box for several minutes, while others looked as if they'd expected more and hurriedly shuffled back down the stairs, shamefaced. I never saw any man pay to look twice.

Before anyone had a chance to notice me as a stranger on the lot, the flaps of a tent wall at the end of the midway lifted up, and West appeared in a sequined purple satin shirt. Alone in the midway, we approached one another. He helped bridge the awkwardness by holding out his hand to take my army duffel and rolled-up tent.

"You came back," he said, showering me with a radiant smile. "I see you've come to stay."

"I brought my own tent, just in case," I said, falling in step with him. We walked away from the circus grounds together, down a dirt road in the moonlight, to look for a good place to camp. He was easy to talk to and didn't stand on ceremony or wait for a sign before plunging into conversation.

"Your parents know you're here?"

"Yup. Just called them."

"They must be pretty broadminded to let you come out here on your own."

"I've been trying to get a summer job for a while."

"That so? You couldn't get a job back where you live?"

I told him about my brief stint as a trainee at the Pewter Pot Muffin House. They'd asked me to show up in a white blouse and black skirt—items hopelessly missing from my hippie wardrobe. I'd promptly soaked one of my purple miniskirts from ninth grade in a boiling pot of black Rit dye. I picked up a filmy white blouse at a discount store because it was so cheap. But the translucency didn't matter because I had a beige bra that matched the color of my tan skin.

The manager was a man in his thirties with thick dark hair and bushy eyebrows; he had looked me over as I entered the Muffin House. "I was sure he was checking to see if I'd remembered to wear the uniform," I told West as we walked along side by side. "I'd memorized the entire menu too." I told the circus boy how slow it had been that day. Very few customers passed through. My feet pinched in the uncomfortable black flats I'd had to wear with the skirt, and all I could do was wish for the shift to end so that I could fly away on my bicycle and feel the whoosh of air rush up my skirt as I pumped past the shops in our sleepy suburban town. "My day ended in absolute failure," I continued. "The manager decided to hire Miss Cheery Bubbly, and I was sent packing. He told me, 'You're just not suitable.'"

"Why was that?" asked West as we marched along. He had that easy, long-legged stride of a tall man used to getting around on foot.

"The manager said I wasn't wearing a bra. But I was—it was flesh colored, that's all."

West smiled to himself as I concluded my story. "Sounds like he could have told you as much before you spent the entire day making him hot!"

"Yeah," I laughed. "Anyway, I got fired before I even got started, and then I got nowhere. I just did chores on a farm for my grandmother. Not a *real* job. What I really want to do is travel, to go somewhere far away and different, like India or Egypt."

West and I followed the dirt path until we came to a grassy field near the sound of rushing water. "Yeah, I'm saving up to travel too," he said. "Circus life is good that way. You get to keep all the money you make because you don't have to pay for room and board. And you travel every day. That's the best."

The circus boy paused and let the tent roll drop to the ground. Methodically, we set to pitching the tent together and made a plan. In order to ride in the circus trucks, I needed to get a job with the circus. Then I could follow the show, sleep in my tent at night, and ride in one of the trucks to the next lot.

"How old are you? I can't be taking any minors across state lines."

"Seventeen, but I can pass for nineteen, I think."

"Seventeen, huh? You don't look that young to me. If anyone asks, you tell them you're nineteen. Okay?" He flicked his eyes over my tall frame, taking in the curves of my body where I had them. "You sure grew up fast. And you have the walk of a full-grown woman."

After we completed the setup, we sat side by side next to the pitched tent and fell silent, faltering at the next steps. Up until that point, I had only savored thoughts of touching his arm or his face. I was hoping that once I arrived, he'd take the reins or at least confirm that he'd been dreaming and thinking about me this whole time too. The air grew heavy with things left unsaid. I had kept my promise to return, and he had told me he would wait for me. But now that we had been reunited, neither one of us seemed willing to hope for too much.

"I have to go back to the lot," he said finally, "change my clothes, and see about the cats." He grabbed my hand, pulling me up off the ground. "Come on, you can get something to eat at the diner while you wait."

We were wading through the warm summer air, shoulder to shoulder again, and I was feeling high, elated because we were striding along like partners. My hair floated off my shoulders in rhythm with the crunching of his steel-toed work boots.

Soda fountain customers gave us quizzical looks when we entered the diner. *Circus people must always turn heads*, I thought. Against the drab wallpaper, West's colorful, sequined clothing certainly stood out. West flipped a roll of bills and gave the waitress a ten.

"She can have whatever she wants," he said, and then he was gone. Alone at the diner, I stirred my coffee, waiting for the shape of his body to reappear at the spot under the street lights where he had disappeared from my view. He was taking a while. I finished my pie and looked out the window at the neon sign of the motel across the road. A candle blinked red, off and on, filling with glowing liquid and then bursting into flame over and over again. I had to smile at myself. I was brimming with anticipation that I could barely contain.

The minutes ticked slowly by. When the Candlelight Motel's neon sign gave a shudder and went out completely, I had one terrible moment of trying very hard not to look at the waitress sponging the counter behind the soda fountain. I kept my head down, busying myself to show signs of imminent departure. Then came the soft tapping at the curtained window by my booth. I got up, gratefully left all the change on the table, and slipped out the screen door, which closed with a bang.

West greeted me in his flak jacket and washed-out red jump-suit with the words *Reyes Bros. Ragtime Gypsy Show* embroidered on the back. Fireflies were out, and they danced over the fields on either side of us as we made our way back to our campsite. We talked some about how the circus hands had caught West pining away and about how my being there was all right with them. They had no problem with picking me up on the road as a hitchhiker for my first jump until West got things straightened out with Monsieur Lefèvre, the circus owner. They needed someone to sew up the tears in the big top, West explained. Someone named Mike had blown the show to go work for a carney.

"Do you think you could do that?"

"Sure. I sew."

"Beats me why Mike left. Carnivals take a lot of riffraff and jailbirds. They don't have any acts, just rides and rigged games. He might make more money in concessions, but that atmosphere attracts a certain kind. It's not like the circus where you have performers. Although to be fair, we have our jailbirds too." The dark-haired young man looked away, as if scanning the riverbank for a sign.

It was getting cold with the wind blowing off the river. West wrapped half of his flak jacket around me to keep me warm, and we huddled together. I picked up the conversation we had left off the very first time we'd met. "So what animals would you take with you to South America?"

"A pair of female elephants," he responded. "Two that like each other, like Bessie and Mary."

"Why not a male and a female?"

"Hell no! You have no idea what a male elephant goes through when he's in his musth phase. Bulls get so horny they become violent—so out of control, they go rogue—and they destroy everything they see."

"It's a phase? Like when a female goes into heat? The males don't just respond to the female's estrus cycle?"

"Oh yeah, they respond all right! During the musth phase, a male elephant will leave his bachelor herd of bulls to seek out a receptive female in the cow herd. You could say it's a mutual thing with elephants. A spike in hormones makes them both fall madly in love, like people, and then they get together and mate. And when they do—watch out! The bull wants it and so does the female. They say it's something spectacular!"

"Perfect. No courtship ritual. No guesswork. I like it," I said.

West leaned back, bracing himself on the ground with his elbows. He laughed in a satisfied way, "I'm sure you do, Miss Sarah."

"Cut it out," I protested. "And what's with this Miss Sarah stuff? I hate being addressed as 'Miss.'"

"Addressed? Oh, so you want to be a Ms.? You're one of them—what do you call them? —goddamn feminist girls with their noses up their fine behinds!" The words were harsh, but I knew he was teasing me. I was used to holding my own with my sarcastic older brothers.

"I don't want to be a Miss Anything. Just Sarah, plain and simple. My name. That's it."

"You're not going to like the South then. Down there it's all 'yes, sir' and 'no, ma'am,' and you'll be called 'Miss Whoever from Massatoosey.'"

We sat on the grass by the river for a while. "If you want, we can just sleep side by side. We don't have to do anything, you know." West looked straight ahead, his hands locked over his bent knees. "If it's not right, it's not right."

"I'm still a virgin," I said.

"That so?" he put his hand to my cheek and brought his face to my lips. "You don't kiss like a virgin."

My army tent smelled of rubber and canvas. The circus boy's worn, working hands moved with authority, and I was surprised at every turn how easy it was to lie together. West was older than most of the boys I'd known, and he was careful with me, as if he expected me to bolt like a frightened filly. He wasn't afraid to talk to me as I braced myself.

"Why are you closing your eyes?" He propped himself up on his elbows and smiled down at me as I lay beneath him.

"I don't know."

"Are you afraid?" The unruly shock of hair fell forward, almost touching my face, as he leaned closer to read my expression.

"No ... no. But I don't really ... know what's going to happen. It might hurt, right?"

"I'll take it easy with you if you can take it easy with me," West laughed.

"Very funny," I couldn't believe he was talking to me. My boyfriend and I had always fooled around in morbid silence.

"It's not as serious as you think," West assured me. "But I want you to really be here with me." The circus boy saw me hesitate. "If this is your first time, you won't want to miss it."

"I don't think I can do this with my eyes open."

"That's okay, but don't be thinking about someone else. That's no good. Not for me or for you."

"Are you kidding?" I jerked my body from beneath him and sat up suddenly. "Since we met, I haven't thought of anyone else."

"Me neither." The circus boy looked at me with joy in his eyes, and we eased back to the ground. "Just making sure you're sure," he whispered in my ear.

West demanded nothing beyond the soothing human comfort of being touched and held. He was letting me decide, I could tell. When, in my shy way, I positioned myself beneath him, he asked, "Are you ready for this?" I closed my eyes and nodded.

Penetration was a surprise, a shock like the meeting of water and stone. He tried to be gentle, even deliberate at first. But as he lost control, our breathing got wilder, and the pieces of me that had been strapped in came undone, splintered. I was obliterated. I didn't exist. I was a vapor, a color, dust catching light.

After we made love, West stroked my hair and spoke to me in a voice full and deep; I had never heard my name spoken in that husky, broken tone before. "Sarah, I want you to be with me. I always want to wake up and find you here, just like this." He was stretched out on his back, and I lay my head on his chest with one arm across his torso.

"I'll follow you, hitchhike, and camp out on every lot if I have to," I said.

Later West would insist that I must have been lying about making love for the first time. I was flattered he had noticed my experience, but, in the dawn, I wanted no doubts. If I had been set on losing my virginity, I wanted him to know that he had been the first. To prove it, we tried to find traces of blood. Not much, but there it was—a stain like raspberry jam.

"Goddamn!" West whispered, caught off guard. He hugged me with a sweet animal tenderness, and we made love again, wide-awake, with our eyes open. I had crossed over. That was all that mattered to me. The ecstatic pleasure part I'd heard so much about wasn't there yet. He told me it would take time; it would come later, when I wasn't so green.

West smuggled breakfast over to our campsite by the river: a cup of black coffee in a Styrofoam cup and store-bought Danish. He was running late and couldn't stay to eat with me; he had to go back to his truck, load the elephants, and pull off the lot. We agreed I should wait for him out on the open road.

"Don't you go getting up in anybody else's cab, you hear?" he cracked a wicked smile, but his eyes were serious. Before I could say a word, he squeezed my hand and then turned and ran off at an easy lope.

★ ★ ★

There I was, biding my time, watching the mist rise off the fields by the side of the road in Bloomsburg, Pennsylvania, with my tent roll and army duffel at my feet. It was a wet, green-grass morning and a too-early feeling scratched behind my eyes. The cookhouse coffee gnawed at my guts. Just knowing that West would be coming down the road shifted all the weights around in my brain so that I felt a happy fatigue, an inner calm that pulled the edges of my lips up into an unconscious smile.

A blast from a truck horn sent a shock through me, and I jumped back. Looking up, I saw the dark, curly head of one of the roustabouts slowing down his painted rig.

"That's all right," I called up to him as he leaned over and opened the cab door with a tattooed arm. "I got a ride coming."

The swarthy man was smiling, jocular. "Name's Deuce. You'll be staying with West then?"

I nodded.

"Then he is one lucky son of a bitch!" he roared and threw his noisy, rattling truck back in gear. West pulled up right behind him, and the two men exchanged meaningful waves.

In this world, I was a lady. West got out and helped me up into the cab, and I slid onto the smooth bench seat beside him. We were together, and within the day, we'd have an unspoken circus marriage. No one would ever try to come between us again.

Barely awake, scenes of our love-making swam before my eyes as the lines on the highway changed from yellow to white to double yellow, and towns, trees, and signs slipped past the open window. I loved holding the memory of our night together in my mind. I could shield my private thoughts from the distractions of daylight and traffic by closing my eyes.

The truck hummed along. West smoked a cigarette and handled the gearshift with lazy movements, his elbow resting on the open window. I was happy, so happy I had finally done it that I kept breaking into senseless laughter.

"You're in a good mood this morning."

"So are you!" I shot back.

"Damn straight," West grinned. "The only problem with staying up all night is I still have to get us to the next lot without having a wreck."

We didn't have CBs then. I don't think our first truck even had a working radio. The throaty roar of the diesel engine was so loud with the windows open that we had to shout. There was a well filled with rumpled blankets to sleep on behind the seats in the cab.

"You get some sleep now while I'm sure I can stay awake," said West as he settled in for the fifty-mile jump to the next town.

"You want me to talk to you?" I played with his long hair at the nape of his neck.

"Nah, just watch my head, and holler at me if you see me nod. I can fall asleep with my eyes open just staring at those double lines. But I'm okay for a while. Sleep now and dream good dreams. We'll be stopping for breakfast soon. Go on."

Dreaming was something I did best. I was always skittering around on the iridescent surface of my fantasies, like a dragonfly across a pond. The hard, deep sleep of men and lions eluded me. Usually I was too restless, like so many circus people, foreign performers, and roustabouts who wanted to stay on the move. But this time, I was barely able to keep my eyes open; my mind wandered off on its own, like an animal set loose in an open field, blissfully untethered. Once I lay my head down on the wadded-up army blanket, I plummeted into a deep sleep.

About an hour later, I woke up when the stronger sunlight of day splashed through the windshield. West hadn't slept at all, and he was beginning to fade. I passed him a lit cigarette to help keep him awake at the wheel.

We talked about life on the road and who was out there riding in the circus trucks. West told me some of the roustabouts were actually on the run from the law, but the circus ringmaster, Monsieur Lefèvre, didn't care. He needed the manpower.

"Moving on—that's what we live for. Everyone is running from something," he said, taking a thoughtful drag on his cigarette. He didn't look at me but just kept on driving, staring ahead down the long gray highway.

"What about you?" I asked, "Are you running too?"

"Why? Did Red tell you something?" West turned his face toward me sharply; a lock of dark hair fell into his eyes. For a moment, I was surprised. His eyes looked stormy, angry even. Did I detect a menacing look? Then, when he focused on the road again, he squinted as he took another pull on his cigarette.

"Red told me they picked you up in Florida and that you'd been living in the swamp. You know, that's why he calls you Tarzan."

"He's right about that. Lived on what I could catch for months."

"How'd you learn to do that?"

"I'm part Seminole Indian. I've been doing that kind of thing since I was eleven: fishing, hunting iguanas and birds with a crossbow and a sling shot. I know how to track animals and be real quiet out in the swamp. That's the only thing my daddy ever taught me before he ditched my momma, and we moved up to Lake City. It's in northern Florida, not far from Deland."

"Isn't that where Reyes Bros. ends the tour?" I had seen the circus business address listed on the route card with a post office box in Deland.

"Yeah, that's right," West began. "Deland is where the circus makes its winter quarters—home to circus bums, drug dealers, and all kinds of misfits. People who keep exotic pets, hunt for gators—all kinds of crazy shit. Close one door and you enter another."

The circus boy fell silent, took a final drag on his cigarette, and turned his attention to the road. Then he chucked the spent filter out the window.

"I hate Sundays," West admitted after a pause. "Nothing takes more out of a man than Sundays. It's supposed to be our day off.

We just stay on the lot an extra day instead of going to a new town. No setup, no teardown, just the shows. The music goes right through your head: same words, same barkers, same damn show. Goddamn days off make me nervous."

I felt the same way. I liked to keep moving and experience new things all the time. Life went stale for me in a day, just like uncovered bread. But circus people had this thing figured out. They all traveled together, and they had each other. They were nomads, real-life gypsies. And now I was a gypsy too. I sneaked a peak at myself in the fish eye of the truck's rearview mirror: dark eyebrows, crazy eyes, hair wrapped in a scarf Hungarian style to keep off the wind.

Over the rise, I saw our caravan of eight painted trucks all lined up by the side of the road. Red and yellow lettering and murals of sensational circus acts covered the full side of the animal trucks. The light truck and the spool truck carrying the big top canvas were parked behind. We drove the elephant truck, which was no easy job when two restless pachyderms weighing four tons each took to swaying back and forth in the trailer.

When the circus roustabouts pulled into the truck stop, they pushed several tables together and took every seat. The circus crew liked to eat family style, passing around bowls of grits and plates of pancakes. Catcalls flew as each man told stories about his previous night's conquest.

They relished their breakfasts, teased one another, and told jokes. I was the only female among the circus working men. West didn't join in with all the roustabouts' loud mouthing off; he just laughed and kept up his end quietly. No one asked what I was doing there. They made me feel special, offering me a seat, showing me to the ladies room.

"Hey, Pops, how'd you make out with the fat lady?" Out the window I saw an obese young woman with dark frizzy hair leaning against the spool truck, filing her nails with an emery board.

"I likes 'em fat; that's the truth." Pops had a round, cartoonish face, and he gave a sheepish smile. "And they like me too!"

"What about your wife?"

"Love her too. Fact is I tried to go and see her last night, just like every year when we come through Bloomsburg."

Red leaned over and explained to me that Pops had a ritual of leaving his suitcase on the porch and ringing the doorbell when he visited his wife while the circus was touring. If she turned on the porch light and took the suitcase in, he would be allowed to spend the night. If not, he was on his own. Sometimes his wife couldn't stand to see him.

"What did she do this year, Pops?"

"Well, I put my suitcase up on the porch, just like always, and then I went and hid in the bushes. This time, she turned on the porch light, but she threw my suitcase clean into the road and slammed the door." There was a wave of feigned surprise. "It's not my fault," said Pops. "I just can't say no to—"

Blacky, the cook, spoke up, "Hey, there's a lady present!" He reminded the crew more than once, especially when the language got ripe.

I took the opportunity to excuse myself. The little dark bathroom had a sink and a mirror, all I needed to put myself back together. But the pieces of my face didn't seem to fall back into place in a familiar pattern. My eyes, with deep circles beneath them, looked sultry, and a hint of sarcasm pulled at the corners of my mouth. But the fleshiness of baby fat still rounded out my chin. I leaned to one side, braided my long brown hair again, refastened my gypsy scarf, and smoothed my long dungaree skirt. Before I'd left, I'd sewn on a border of patchwork from India at the hem of the skirt. It looked like the awning of a fortuneteller's tent.

Making my way back to the table, I wandered by the booths where the performers were taking their seats. They were arriving just as the roustabouts were leaving, not under pressure to reach the lot early for setup.

West stood up as I approached the long table, now abandoned by the crew. A pile of dirty dollar bills had been stacked neatly among the empty plates. The mid-morning sun came in through the frilly restaurant curtains, heating up the orange juice left in the glasses.

As we walked outside, I felt the circus boy's arm grip my waist, hand on my hipbone. He was claiming me, right there. Smiling and talking about everything but the obvious, the roustabouts nodded knowingly at West before climbing back into their cabs. I was West's girl now.

THE ELEPHANT WHISPERER

he circus owner and ringmaster, Monsieur Lefèvre, was a shrewd, short man from France, who got by just fine in the South speaking Cajun French. Someone said that he'd trained to be a lion tamer with the Clyde Beatty Show before running his own show as ringmaster for the Reyes Bros. Ragtime Gypsy Show. There were also whispers that the show was running at a loss as a tax write-off for the mob in Tampa. I didn't understand how money laundering worked, and all I knew about the New England Mafia was secondhand information from my father when he occasionally looked up from his newspaper and declared, "Disgraceful. Another gangland slaying in South Boston."

The whole affair was edgy, like my after-dark visits to Boston's red-light district in Chinatown with my boyfriend by my side to keep me clear of the johns. And now that I was being smuggled into a traveling circus, I relied once again on a man—West—as the ally and protector of my secret adventures.

★ ★ ★

As soon as we reached the circus grounds in South Williamsport, the circus boy hopped out of the truck cab and hustled across the midway in search of Lefèvre, the Napoleon-sized

French ringmaster. I watched West from a distance as he leaned his elbows on the counter outside the screened ticket window of the office truck. Negotiations went on for some time. The circus boy eventually rested his chin on stacked fists and peered into Mr. Lefèvre's narrow face as he insisted and finally persuaded him to let me join the canvas crew. I would be paid twenty-five dollars a week to join as a roustabout to help with morning setup and then sew up any tears in the tent before lunch. A job meant that I could take my meals at the cookhouse, ride in the trucks, and sleep in a bunk bed with West in the elephant truck. And work would start immediately.

While we waited for the pole truck to arrive, we waded through the grass to West's sleeper, one of the painted trucks along the midway used to transport two Indian elephants that rocked the semitrailer when they were chained up inside for the night. During the day, Bessie and Mary were staked out close to their truck with a big oil drum filled with water within reach of their roving trunks.

West hopped up on the engine behind the truck cab and reached up to the metal door handle on the front corner of the truck trailer. He opened the door on a narrow windowless barracks room with an army-style bunk bed and a wooden floor. Then he hoisted himself inside from his crouched position on the engine. Inside the sleeper, propped up against the wall, was a metal ladder painted white, a castoff from one of the aerial acts. West hauled out the ladder and began to lower it to the ground. I reached up, grabbed the rungs and took it from him easily before steadying the ladder at the base, digging its feet into the dirt. Then I propped it against the open door, a gaping dark hole standing above the truck tire about five feet from the ground—too high up for me to climb into without a boost.

"Can I come up yet?" I could only make out the metal frame of the bunk bed against the truck wall.

"Not ready for you yet." West looked irritated.

I turned my back. I was getting tired of being told what to do. Suddenly I was hit by a flying pile of dirty sheets, blankets, and pillows that knocked me over.

"You can come up now, sweet Sarah."

"Come down and get me." On my back on the heap of bedclothes, I propped myself up on my elbows. In one huge leap from the truck, he was next to me. He held himself over me on all fours and kissed me back to the ground. I was soon laughing again. I could feel myself floating away as he pressed close.

"Someone else was using my sleeper last night while I was busy with you," West explained.

"What the hell?" I rolled off the soiled bedding and jumped to my feet.

"Now, don't be like that. Not everybody has a sleeper. A lot of guys just sleep in the cab of the truck or even bed down in the hay with the elephants. *I've* done it! We share a good bed when we get a chance to catch a little loving."

"I'll get new sheets in town. This is our place now," I said, glaring at him.

"Yes, ma'am," he teased, but he was pleased with himself. West picked me up off my feet and twirled me around in his arms before setting me down on the ground.

Once I clambered up into the sleeper, I fell in love with it for its old-timey appeal. A small four-by-six-foot living space had been partitioned off by soldering a makeshift wall between the container and the sleeper. On the other side of the sleeper wall, taking up the rest of the truck container, were the elephants in an open stall of hay. The metal walls of the sleeper had been left bare, but a floor had been laid down with uneven wooden planks. The splintered wood displayed open cracks filled with animal dust and hay. A small rope was strung up in the corner for hanging West's fancy costumes. The rest of his clothes and belongings were in an old antique bureau with a spotted mirror. That was the only piece of furniture in the narrow living space, other than the bunk bed, which was pushed up flush against a metal wall too hot to touch by midday. There was no running water and no bathroom. The only light source came from a kerosene lamp on the dresser. The mirror helped reflect the glowing light, and I was enchanted by it all. I had gone back in time without leaving the country.

I unpacked my few things into the empty spaces in the bureau. I also added some domestic touches to the trailer: a cloth hanging of an open palm, mapped out with lines and mounts for fortune-telling; a calendar featuring a picture of Ganesh; and a colorful patterned Indian bedspread. I had brought all these things with me in an old army duffel bag to fuel my fantasies of living as a wanderer and a gypsy. This sleeper was my home now.

★ ★ ★

"West! Get your goddamn ass over here!" It was Red, the circus elder who still held on to his position as canvas boss in spite of his age. "I said, West! Where is that crazy swamp rat?" Red muttered to himself as he set up a folding chair on the grass at the sideshow entrance in the midway where he made his headquarters.

We were headed in Red's direction so that I could meet Lefèvre in person at the office truck and get signed on as a roustabout. West slowed his pace as we came up behind the ringmaster's truck and signaled to me to crouch down behind the trailer. We watched with barely muffled amusement as old man Red searched for a level spot on the ground for his folding chair on the opposite side of the midway. West was just about to spring out from behind the office truck and surprise the old man when we heard voices and the rattle of a wooden drawer opening and closing from within the manager's truck.

The circus boy smiled at me. "That's got to be Lefèvre, counting up all his money first thing in the morning."

Then we heard a young woman's voice carry through the open screen of the ticket window. "I hear Humberto plans to blow the show and take up with a carnival. You think West could do the elephant act on his own? He already knows the routine."

The circus boy put a finger to his lips and mouthed the words, "Brigitte, Lefèvre's oldest daughter." He made a face and squared his shoulders in imitation of her imperious attitude.

Lefèvre answered in his French accent, dropping his h's. "I don't know. Don't ask me till it happens. As long as Humberto stays, we have an elephant trainer. After that, I don't know." The ringmaster's voice became high-pitched with irritation. "This happens every year when a carney sets up nearby. Lazy performers like Humberto think they can make more money gambling or by giving pony rides. I don't know what he's thinking; he can go to hell for all I care!" The manager's voice died away when he turned his back to the window.

West's eyes never left the spot across the midway where Red sat in silence, scanning the grounds for the sight of him. The circus boy began to stand up slowly and revealed himself from behind the truck tire, as if realizing it was becoming too risky to continue eavesdropping by the manager's trailer with Red on the lookout for him.

I heard the old man laughing softly. "Get over here, West!" he hollered. "You too, Miss Sarah!" We had no time to worry about being seen; we ducked behind a few trailers and raced down the midway. Red had his folding chair in his hands, ready to swing at West by the time we reached him at the sideshow marquee.

"What took you so goddamn long, boy? The elephants need watering before some candy ass takes a bath in one of them barrels and soaps up the water. Can't give elephants soapy water, you know."

"Sorry, Red," West said, hands raised high in mock self-defense.

"Like hell, you're sorry." The old man gave me a sidelong glance. When he caught me looking at him, he lunged forward, bugged his eyes out at me, and hooted.

"Hey, come on, Red. I only been on the lot twenty minutes," the circus boy complained.

"How'd you like to clean up after the elephants get the runs?" A smile played at West's lips.

"Listen here, West." Red looked the boy in the eye, his face tilted to one side. "Them animals don't get to ask for a cup of coffee. When it comes right down to it, the goddamn tigers eat better than we do. Just see Lefèvre toss us a couple of day-old steaks! So when we get to a new lot, you got to take care of the animals first; then go get your coffee." Even though he was talking to West, I knew he was making the rules of the game plain to me. I could not become a distraction. Even so, I was relieved that Red hadn't figured out what we'd been up to, eavesdropping by the manager's truck.

"Okay. Okay." West eased himself behind an empty oil drum and rolled it down the midway to the back yard—the place prohibited to circus-goers—where the chained elephants were playing with the loose, dry dirt. While he filled the barrel with water, Mary and Bessie flapped their ears back and forth and uttered affectionate creaking noises. I was quick to make myself useful by following West with the second empty oil drum, and the old man limped behind me down the concourse.

When we joined the circus boy, Red eased himself down on a hay bale, lifted a ragged arm, and pointed to the larger elephant. "Did you see what happened to Mary?" A deep cut on the top of the elephant's ear was clayed over with dried blood. West let the hose fall into the barrel.

"Goddamn that Humberto! Can't he get through a show without tearing her ear off with the bull hook? Where's the iodine, Red? Goddamn him to holy hell!"

West was always so quiet. I had never seen him get this worked up. Red jerked his head in the direction of his truck cab and remained seated with splayed knees on the bale of hay. He called out after West, "Maybe that's why Humberto the Magnificent gets to perform in the ring, and you're out here shoveling shit!"

West reached in the truck and extracted a purple glass bottle with a stopper in it from the glove compartment. When he turned back to face us, the circus boy looked at Red without speaking. I was amazed to see how angry West had become over this incident. His body became dangerously still, as if he was ready to attack at any moment. To an outsider, he might have appeared absolutely calm and at ease. But I knew he wasn't. His demeanor was unsettling.

Red got up and hobbled over to the barrels to steady the hose. "Control! Control! Humberto has been fighting all season to control them elephants. And nobody is going to get anywhere near them without the bull hook now."

West looked down and moistened a cotton ball with the purple disinfectant. "Sure, beat the hell out of them. Sure, sure." He daubed the iodine over the wound, and the elephant flinched suddenly, raising her massive head.

"Easy, Mary." West's shoulders relaxed as he soothed the injured elephant. All his tension seemed to melt away as swiftly as it had appeared. While the circus boy stroked the elephant's hairy hide, he asked the old man, "Are you putting me up to something, Red?"

The white-haired man opened his mouth and gasped before he wheezed out a soundless laugh that left him breathless. Tears came to his eyes, and he began to cough. He walked stiff-legged a few paces, fumbled for purchase on another hay bale, and sat down. "I'll make a circus bum out of you yet, you old swamp rat!" he choked.

"Aw, come on, Red. I can't see how a bull man is any good if he has to rip them open." West stalked over to the second barrel with the hose and began to fill it.

"I can see you got your own ideas about training animals," countered Red. "The circus don't give a goddamn about what you think. All they care about is putting on a show. Everybody knows how you feel about them elephants. You sleep with them;

you talk to them; you take them to the river; you keep little kids from feeding them rocks. You know what the roustabouts are calling you now?"

"No, what?"

"Tarzan!" Red rasped out another painful cackle.

West unchained the elephants and led them over to the water barrels. "I heard that Humberto is going to work for a carney," ventured West.

"You heard right. He's blowing the show, and Lefèvre is not going to do the act for him."

"So what am I supposed to do, Red?"

"Get to work, goddammit! Don't just stand around like a scarecrow. If you want to be the one to take over the elephant act, you got to train the elephants in the ring every day in between shows. I'll make sure Lefèvre gets a look."

"Thanks, Red."

"'S all right, Tarzan!"

★ ★ ★

Soon enough, even I was allowed to handle the elephants when they were cordoned off on display at the sideshow. But it could be tricky when West was nearby. The elephants were in love with him. Once, when West and I walked up to them with our arms around each other, Mary, the older one, wrapped her trunk around West's broad shoulders and gave him a hug right in front of me. I was delighted when the other female elephant, Bessie, curled her trunk around my waist and pulled me toward her.

All of a sudden, West shouted, "Foot up, Bessie!" and released himself quickly from Mary's embrace. "Get back, Sarah!"

The elephant's foot hovered in the air inches above mine.

"She's going to step on you!"

I jumped back in surprise, losing a sandal. It would have been so easy for her to crush all the bones in my foot.

"What a dirty trick! They hate me." I watched in shock as the four-ton elephant slowly brought her raised foot back to the ground.

"Well, maybe they do," West laughed. "I guess we can't be carrying on kissing and hugging in front of them. Maybe it's best not to make them jealous."

"Yeah, guess not." I stood several paces away from West with my arms folded across my chest and stared the elephant in the eye. Her one eye was merry, laughing inside behind a sheet of long lashes. I wasn't used to reading the emotions of such a large, slow animal.

"How can I get them to like me?" I asked.

West showed me how to caress their tongues and scratch inside their ears. They bobbed their heads and made creaking sounds when they were pleased and flapped their ears and snorted when they were annoyed or excited. Most of the time, they were content to explore the ground with their roving trunks, picking up whatever they found to taste it.

"When an elephant gets mad at you, she'll use her trunk. Red told me that some fresh guy tried feeding rocks to the elephants out of a peanut bag. Bessie coiled up her trunk like a spring and threw him a punch that knocked him clear across the sideshow and through a tent wall. That trunk is all muscle. And their tails aren't just tails; they can hit you as hard as a hammer. So you got to be careful. Elephants look slow, but they're smart."

Once Humberto left, it wasn't long before Red convinced the ringmaster to let West take over as the new elephant trainer. With West in charge, Bessie and Mary had more freedom, and they were allowed to wander about without foot chains for long periods of time. The circus boy could call them to him like dogs, and they would come thundering across the circus grounds to meet him. "Come, Bessie. Come, Mary," West's deep voice would carry across the length of a football field. No one else could do it. It was his gift.

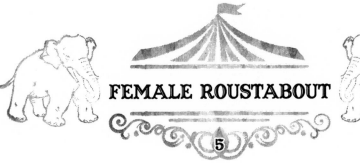

FEMALE ROUSTABOUT

5

he work wasn't difficult to learn, and setup and teardown didn't even seem hard to do at first, after all those summers in New Hampshire hauling brush and tossing hay bales up into the truck alongside my brothers on the farm. Handing poles off the truck and shouldering one or two around the lot was easy, mechanical. I kept working, even while the young circus hands squatted over their work boots in the dirt guzzling Cokes from the concession stand. Some smoked for a while. I kept hauling and dumping tent poles, and I even carried out the heavy metal center pole with Jesse and a few of the older men. I got along fine with the canvas crew, but it was never clear to me why the roustabouts' friendliness only went so far. I would catch them watching me with a hint of amusement, as if they were in on a secret, one that I would never be privy to.

"Come on, let's get this thing done!" Jesse called out in his rich Alabama drawl. He looked rough and handsome, like a stunt man for a spaghetti western. I liked him a lot for his direct hit way of talking. He liked me well enough except that I was a "goddamn Yankee." I made sure to pick up a southern accent fast around him. At Jesse's table at the cookhouse, the talk was all about how the South would have won the Civil War if it hadn't been sold out and about how Robert E. Lee was a better general, southerners better soldiers, and on and on until there were only two people left spooning their lime green Jell-O: Jesse and the cook, Blacky.

A clown named Pops was in charge of rounding up the curious townie boys and lot lice to help pull open the tent in exchange for free tickets to the show. I spied Pops with them, huddled together, talking strategy like a junior football team. Stationed three feet apart, with as many as twenty of us all lined up with an edge of big top canvas held tightly in our hands, we pulled, taking big swinging strides together, stretching the tent across the grassy lot.

Next, we positioned the poles, aiming their metal tips into round reinforced grommet holes in the tent sidewall, and then we threw the pole upright by gripping it and lunging forward. Later, we secured the tent poles in place with the same yellow ropes I had ducked under the night I joined the circus. Jesse and his crew would come around with sledge hammers and pound stakes into the ground until the guy lines were secure.

During one setup, I heard West's familiar voice booming in the distance, commanding the elephants, "Move up, Bessie!" The center pole was going up, but when the canvas sky billowed, something was not quite right. In the center, at the tent's apex, a tear had worked itself into a hole the size of my fist.

"It can't stay like that. Got to get that goddamn hole mended. Hold up!" Jesse hollered and ran a hand through his thick hair, which was cut in a country boy jelly roll in the style of Johnny Cash. The crew broke for lunch, a nice long rest for the roustabouts who had been smoking. They ambled over to the cookhouse, and I made to follow, but Jesse had me stay behind to sew.

"Let's see if your Yankee ass is good for something," he cracked a smile and left me alone with my sewing gear on the flattened surface of the big top tent.

The tent blanketed over the freshly-mown grass in a pool of canvas, wrinkled in places like a deflated hot air balloon. I could see why mending rips was no work for a roustabout trying to throw off a hangover. The noonday sun beat down hard, and my head pounded. The needle was five inches long, and I struggled to push it through the tough canvas. I was grateful for the hand thong with its heavy leather heel. The center pole opening was mended and secure after an hour of double-whip stitching. I then reinforced everything with a running stitch.

Lunch was over by the time I finished, but I managed to get some canned peaches in a light green plastic dish. Blacky, the burly cook who never wore his shirt but used it to mop his hairy chest and underarms by the stove instead, kept me company. He put away the dishes he'd washed up in an oil drum full of water while I spooned the peaches into my mouth. The fruit syrup tasted faintly of detergent.

"Got a lot of government issue," Blacky offered.

"Yeah, just like at school."

"You a schoolgirl?

"Not anymore. All finished," I said. It was true that I'd graduated early from high school, but I wasn't sure if I was up for going to college right away. I wanted a taste of the real world and a real job. Now that I'd landed one, I would have time to figure things out.

The hefty cook didn't press me. "You're from cold country. I just can't stand the snow. That's why I spend winters in Florida. But you got some great roads in New Hampshire. We all can't wait to get there when we start out. Some beautiful roads," Blacky mused, wiping down the stove. "You wait now, and you'll see. Once we get going through the mountains in Tennessee and the Carolinas, we'll all be praying the brakes are working. Lots of wrecks happen on those roads. Lot of things can go wrong." Blacky struck a pose in the doorway of the cookhouse truck, arm over his head, as if he was hanging one-handed from the branch of a tree. He seemed to drift off somewhere, conjuring up a loved one in his mind, I guessed.

"Are you married?" I asked.

"Yep. Got my wife in Florida. I know something about what you got going with West. You think you two are in love? You wait a while. That's nothing. Twenty-two years of marriage. Now that's love—real love. You take it from old Blacky here."

Things with West had happened so fast, and here, at the circus, no one blinked an eye. People fell in love, and everyone formed a sacred, protective circle around the lovers. It had taken me two years of note passing, phone calls to girlfriends, and diary writing—not to mention seven months of lingering nonchalantly outside classroom doors and lockers—just to get my boyfriend to use the word *love* in a conversation. "How could I have known you were in love with me?" he'd said when I'd waited for him in freezing rain after school. "What do you think I am, psychic?"

I had fallen into another world at the circus, where time was foreshortened. There was only now, this moment in time. The season only lasted so long. The route card followed the summer sun from north to south, ending in Deland, Florida, by Halloween. Then the performers would spend the winter touring indoor arenas with the big shows, like Barnum and Bailey, if they could swing it. They said they hated the cold cement walls crushing the sequins on their backs as they waited to go on. A lot of performers lived in their trailers all winter, and some roustabouts picked up truck-driving jobs until the circus season started again.

But not Blacky. He owned a boat and liked to go fishing and spend time with his wife. He was the only truly peaceful person I had met at the circus. It was easy to take his advice when he said, "You go easy with West. I know he likes you a lot. Don't break his heart—at least not while I'm around. Okay?"

★ ★ ★

A week went by, and our ranks diminished briefly as a few hands, following Humberto's lead, left to join a carney. But the circus attracted all kinds; before long, we managed to pick up a few new guys in Ohio.

"Hey, Sarah," the circus boy called out to me from center ring as I entered the big top to rope the poles. "We just got a new truck driver, a kid from Massatoosey, like you. That's him, Dave."

Dave didn't remind me of any of the guys I knew in Massachusetts. His looks were confusing. *If he washed his long, stringy hair and lost the red acne blotches that pebbled his face, he could be attractive, even devastating,* I thought, *like Jim Morrison of The Doors.* He had a skinny rock star body; only a two-inch thick belt added dimension to his waist.

This new kid looked young to me. Dave moved around easily and could swing a sledge hammer, but he lacked the build in his upper body that distinguished the older roustabouts as men. I wondered if he was really old enough to drive truck. Maybe I was even a little worried he'd take my spot on the crew.

"Hey, Massatoosey," Dave greeted me briefly and leaned on the handle of his sledge hammer.

"Hey, Yankee. You got a license to drive these rigs?" I was trying to imitate the tough talk I heard every day to make it clear to Dave that I was one of the roustabouts.

"Maybe. Who's asking?" Dave was quick to dish it right back.

"Come on, Sarah. Don't give Dave a hard time. He just got here," West interceded. "What's wrong with you northern types? You always got to be putting each other down."

"You're from Boston?" the new boy looked at me with the steady glare of an adolescent. I noticed the intensity of his eyes, which were dark blue with long lashes.

"Yeah, close enough," I said absently. I didn't want anyone to find out I was from a wealthy family whose ancestors hailed from England and crossed the ocean on the *Mayflower.* No one needed to know where I came from. I had already adopted a casual, laconic way of speaking to hide my identity.

Sizing up this new boy, I began to reimagine his face in my mind, retouching his image like a photographer. When his skin cleared up, he was going to be the smoldering type, with full red lips and a penetrating stare.

When West caught me gawking at him, he became very active, bobbing and weaving like a marionette, vying for my attention. He asserted his authority by rattling off instructions to Dave, "When you get to a weigh station, you got to get out and let Deuce drive on through. That way, they won't check your papers."

"So you *don't* have a license," I said to Dave with a smirk.

West cut me off. "Why don't you head over to the pie car and get us a soda?" He pronounced "soda" as "sodey" like everyone else from winter quarters.

"What you got?" asked Dave, still standing in a casual attitude in his rumpled jeans and Frye boots. His shirt was unbuttoned, and he wore it half in, half out. *It wouldn't be long before he'd lose the shirt altogether,* I thought, *and then he'd wash the dirt and saw-dust off his back after setup like the rest of the roustabouts.* I caught West looking at me, evaluating my interest in this newcomer. I decided to feign a little hostility toward Dave to cover my tracks.

"Who says I'm going to get you anything? You think I'm some kind of waitress?" I wasn't going anywhere for anyone anyway. I belonged on the setup crew with the guys.

"Oh yeah, I forgot." West leaned over and whispered at Dave's shoulder, looking at me with an amused expression, "She's no good at waitressing. She got fired for showing her tits."

My head shot up. I was so outraged that tears sprang to my eyes, and I turned away from them, fuming, and walked stiffly toward the big top exit.

Behind me I heard Dave chuckle. "Sounds to me like she's real good at it!"

"Mass-hole!" I shot back over my shoulder at Dave, and I stomped off through the uncut grass, headed straight for our truck, and clambered up the ladder into the sleeper.

In a fit of rage, I packed up all my clothes, tore the calendar with the picture of Ganesh from the wall, and made a show of marching off the lot, but no one was around to take notice. The roustabouts were under the big top, and the performers were all busy setting up housekeeping at their makeshift campground over at the performers' row. I could hear the white Eskimo dogs yelping with joy as their master, Fritz, set up their dog run outside his camper. The Palmieri family would be setting up a trampoline and a tightrope outside their door for their children to practice on. *Everyone had their place in the circus world, everyone but me,* I thought.

I hid myself at a distance for as long as I could hold out, chucking my tent and army duffel into an old house foundation. Eventually I climbed a tree to spy on the arrangement of painted trucks and canvas in the distance. West never came looking for me, even as the sun reached its zenith in the sky. I knew setup was over.

Circus pennants fluttered in the breeze at the three highest points on the big top roof. Already I missed being part of the show. I didn't really want to leave; I just wanted West to feel sorry for what he did. I wanted him to know that I could leave at any time if he ever put me down or treated me poorly again. Smells of hamburgers and hot dogs wafted through the air, and a cloud of chatter rose up from the cookhouse. I was missing out on lunch too. I gave up on the charade and dragged my dunnage back to the lot, still put out, but not boiling over.

Back on the lot, I spotted Red in his folding chair surrounded by discarded milk cartons at the edge of the midway. He got up unsteadily and approached me with his uneven gait, rocking back and forth, waving a hand at me. "What are you all hot and bothered about?"

"West makes me so mad! He seems to think he can boss me around like I'm his servant or something." I dropped my gear at my feet, exhausted from the hot, dusty trek back to the lot.

"Now you know West is not like that. You probably spooked him—made him bite you back out of fear." Red picked up my army duffel and made a beeline for his folding chair.

"Fear of what? He's not afraid of me at all," I replied, scurrying behind him, dragging my cumbersome tent roll.

"Hmm." Red looked doubtful. "He loves you. That's all I

know." He let my army duffel drop to the ground and sat down in his chair with a groan of relief. "And that's something you're going to have to handle."

"Well, that doesn't mean he can treat me like shit. He's being so mean to me," I insisted and sat down on a hay bale next to the old man.

"Let me put it this way: you make a man jealous, and something starts to eat him up inside, making him act in crazy ways," said Red, and he took another swig from his milk carton. "You have no idea what a man goes through when he sees his woman looking at another man. That kind of crazy drove me to drink. Hell! Now I've got an ulcer that won't quit in this life or the next!"

That gave me pause. It did add up. Dave had something that attracted me, but he wasn't West and never would be. All the other men on the show knew the rules. I was West's girl—no messing around. But the boy from Massachusetts hadn't been on the lot for a full day yet, and he didn't know he had to keep his eyes in his head. Dave would have his chance one day with some townie girl, just not with any of the beautiful women on the lot in their glittering costumes and made-up faces. They were all taken. And I was too, I guess. Maybe. I wondered what would happen if I changed my mind.

"Did West hit you?" asked Red, lifting his chin as he looked at me with narrowed eyes.

"No! No, of course not," I said, a little taken aback.

"Then he's not mean, just crazy—crazy like you." He began to sing a little song to himself. "Can I sleep in your barn tonight ..." To me, Red was an enigma.

Then I caught sight of West. He was talking animatedly with Alana and Carla, the acrobat twins, and they listened with delicate smiles and nodded their heads. He pretended not to see me and followed them to their camper on the performers' row. This fight was becoming a war.

★ ★ ★

When West and I finally faced each other back at our trailer, it was almost time for the four o'clock show. "I knew you weren't really leaving," he said. "You left your camera behind, hanging from the bed post."

"It's busted anyway; the film won't advance." I was sullen. Nothing I'd tried had made a dent in his attitude toward me. He had won this round. "So you think I was just going off to make you worry?"

"How the hell should I know what dumb things you'll do to get attention? You're worse than that grandstander, Celeste, and she's thirteen."

"So you think I'm a brat."

"I *know* you are! My funny, hard-loving, lovely little wild thing." West's eyes were shining, and he brushed my hair aside with tenderness and slowly pulled me close. "Please," he whispered into my ear, "don't *ever* do that again." He held me with a gentleness that made me quake with relief.

"I can't. I just can't go back to being alone," he said. "You don't know how many nights out in the swamp I wondered if I was going to wake up dead, and no one would ever know."

I pulled away from his embrace to look him in the eye. "How long were you out there, living like that?"

"Two years, I think."

"Two years? Why? That's insane."

"Not if you're me—not if you grow up in a trailer park with a drunk mother, no money, and no future. The minute you turn eighteen, the Selective Service calls you up, and you get a front row seat in Vietnam."

I made the calculation. If he was twenty now, he would have left for the swamp two years ago.

"You're a draft dodger," I said.

"I am. I'm not the only one working here who's hiding out either."

"Dave too?"

"What can I tell you? There are things it's best you don't know, just in case the cops come sniffing around asking questions."

"And West isn't your real name either, is it?"

"Case closed. Who are you anyway? Perry Mason?" West placed his hands on his knees and made to stand up.

I couldn't let it go. "Is that why you get paid in cash, and I don't?" All my payroll earnings as a roustabout were accumulating in the circus bank. I couldn't cash out and get paid in full until we reached winter quarters.

"Look, some of what we do has to look legal. We got so many jailbirds who have jumped parole that there's practically no one on the canvas crew but circus veterans, like Red and Blacky, who can call themselves clean. So, yeah, some of us prefer cash. But you'll probably get a cashier's check with your name on it when we get back to Florida."

"And the ringmaster? Lefèvre is okay with all this?"

"Oh, the performers are all straight arrows," West assured me, looking at me in the mirror as he readied himself for the elephant act. "It's the canvas crew that's full of misfits and outlaws with phony names."

I must have looked terrified. I could feel my eyes telegraphing the fear that pierced my insides. It was a sinking feeling, as if my intestines were slowing filling with ice.

"Oh come on, Sarah," West cajoled me. "No one here is going to slit your throat. They're just a bunch of guys who need to lay low for a while. Guys who made mistakes: gamblers, petty thieves, maybe some longhairs caught with a couple of joints. No big deal. Down South, you get thrown in jail for sewing the American flag on your back pocket—you know that." He turned around and leaned against the antique bureau, facing me as I sat on the bottom bunk.

"What about you? Are you planning to hide out forever?" I asked.

"Me? No chance! Lefèvre and I made a deal. If I help him out with the elephant act this season, he'll teach me all he knows about handling big cats. He was a lion tamer with Clyde Beatty, you know. Then, like I told you, I'm going to get some animals of my own and go to South America and start up my own gig. I'm saving up. It could be a year from now."

He paused and then brought himself down to my eye level. While crouching in front of me, he placed his elbows on my knees and looked into my eyes. "And I want you to come too."

"What?"

"Think about it. Not as a dream but as something you could really do with your life. With me."

"But I don't know how to do any circus tricks," I protested, bewildered by his offer.

"Everybody starts somewhere. Here, practice with these." West pulled three juggling clubs out of a zippered case and showed them to me; they looked like bowling pins with long swanlike necks.

"Where did you get these?" I asked, smiling up at him.

"The acrobat twins. They're on loan for a while, till you learn. You're pretty, you know that? You could be my bally girl. Anyway, you're one of us now," he said and kissed me, leaning into me and pressing closer and closer until I fell over backward on our bunk bed laughing. The shimmering pleasure I had felt on my first morning jump returned. We'd had our first fight and survived.

UNDER THE BIG TOP

6

here was one other circus girl on the lot like me. Margarita wasn't a performer, a member of the boss's family, or a townie who rode with a roustabout for a day or two. She came from the Canary Islands; she was short and fiery and had dyed her hair red with henna. She ran a toy stand in the midway with all the other concessionaires who sold popcorn, cotton candy, and soft drinks out of their trucks along the grassy corridor that led to the big top entrance.

I watched Margarita's petite body strut down the midway in hot pants, a halter top, and high-heeled platform step-ins. Her tanned back was strong, and I wondered if she had ever trained as an acrobat.

"No, not me, honey," she confided in her hoarse Spanish accent. "I was a Playboy bunny before I came here." Reaching under the counter of her concession stand, she retrieved a well-worn porno paperback and pulled out the photo she was using as a bookmark. The black-and-white photograph showed a much younger Margarita in the nude, striking a cabaret-style pose while seated on a bar stool, a feather boa draped over one shoulder and between her legs. Her enormous breasts were on display, but her face was coyly shielded by a wig of long blond hair, and she peered out beneath a fringe of peroxide bangs with a bruised pout.

"Oh yes, I had to have a breast reduction. Can you imagine? My *ta-tas* were too big, even for the Playboy Club!" I could easily imagine her wearing the little cottontail on the tip of her tailbone, leaning over just so, and taking a drink order in her earthy voice.

Deuce came by the toy shack and caught a good look at Margarita's round little ass in her hot pants. Then his eyes fell on the image of a bare-breasted woman on the cover of her sexy paperback. "What're you doing reading all that dirty stuff, Margarita?" he smirked.

The Spanish woman rounded on him with a bold smile, yelling like a fishwife in her raspy voice, "Love is beautiful! Is *not* dirty at all! Making love is *wonderful! You* should do it! *Everybody* should do it!" The gap between her teeth showed in flashes when she laughed. Deuce tromped off, swatting the air with one hand in disgust.

I knew she and I needed to have boyfriends in order to survive life on the road with the roustabouts. The second we let go of the men we slept with there would be a feeding frenzy. I also knew I had to become accepted as a circus roustabout and work alongside the canvas men putting up the tent. It was the only way to stay on as a circus employee. The ringmaster said I needed the insurance in order to ride shotgun up in the truck cab with West as we traveled south.

★ ★ ★

On a blazing night in early August, I came down with a fever so fierce that I had auditory hallucinations. I thought I heard a call for help and left my bed, sleepwalking. In a daze, I wandered around the lot and caught sight of Jesse sleeping under the light truck, one arm flung out to the side and legs splayed wide. In my dream, I sensed the truck was crushing him. When I woke up, I found myself leaning up against the light truck in the dark, shaking as beads of cold sweat streamed from my forehead. My hands were pushing hard against the light truck trailer as I struggled to upend the truck to free Jesse. Soundlessly, West crept up behind me and put a blanket over my shoulders. "Come on, Sarah. Come back to bed."

After only two weeks of working as a roustabout doing setup and teardown, I was forced to quit. I had been over-eager, lifting pole after pole onto my shoulder and roping tent poles while everyone else was idle. The other circus hands just sat on their haunches and smoked, taking their ease, muttering a lazy stream of male banter. At noon every day at the cookhouse, they put their heads down and ate while I baked in the sun, mending the center-hole tear in the big top tent. Hot rays bounced off yards of white canvas laid out on the ground; I was a black dot in a circle of white heat.

West made several attempts to convince Lefèvre to give me another job, but each time he leaned into the office ticket window to make his case, he came away with an earful of "not my problem." West even threatened to leave the show; he pressed his advantage as the sole remaining elephant trainer after Humberto left the circus for the carney. Lefèvre responded with a tirade in French, but the message downshifted to "fix it yourself." Hours later, West returned to our sleeper where I was languishing in the bottom bunk. He arranged a plastic bag filled with ice cone shavings on my forehead and sat down on the edge of the bed.

"Everyone is making like I don't belong here." I was exhausted, too tired to put the energy into crying, so the tears just rolled out by themselves.

West responded without hesitation, "No one belongs here. We're all a big bunch of misfits. Don't let them get to you."

"You think it's okay? Me being a Yankee? Jesse acts like I should be tarred and feathered and left by the side of the road."

"Nah, Jesse is just a hardass. He loves to shoot off his big mouth. But I'm telling you, he likes you. He sees how you just keep on working while the other roustabouts screw around during setup."

I smiled to myself. No one had ever complimented me on my work before. Back on the farm, no matter what it was—hauling brush, dragging fence posts, painting the barn—the job was never done to anyone's satisfaction. It was work that needed doing, carried out by an inept teenager. With three strong, capable older brothers, I was a female afterthought.

West caught me in the act of drifting. He reached for me, gripped my hand in his, and pulled me up off the bed until we stood face to face. Then he put his arms around me and relaxed into a loose embrace. "Don't worry about what anybody thinks or says about what you're doing here." He gave my waist a squeeze. "Fuck 'em."

"Fuck 'em. Yeah," I agreed, but without conviction.

"I like you. You got that in your head?" The circus boy held me close and softly rapped his knuckles on my skull and kept on tapping until he coaxed a full smile out of me.

"I like you too," I said, and I leaned the full weight of my aching head on his shoulder.

"I think we got you another job anyway," he said. "Margarita is going to hire you to sell her toys in the ring, so she can run the toy stand out in the midway and catch the blowoff crowd when people leave the big top. You can keep twenty percent of the money you take in." He handed me a change apron with four pockets.

Because I was feeling better in the cool of the early evening, I allowed West to walk me over to the performers' row. It was the section of mobile homes where the aerialists, acrobats, and jugglers made their camp, far away from the arrangement of painted trucks along the midway where the roustabouts slept in the cabs or containers of their semitrailers. The fortunate few (like us) had beds in a sleeper with a door that could close but not lock.

Margarita took me to the back of her small mobile home camper and showed me a deep carton of toys containing dozens of small stuffed animals that I would have to tie onto a T-stick one by one.

"What about this one?" It was an oversized stuffed bear, with a head the size of a basketball. "Too big, I guess." I grinned at her.

"Too big is *never* a problem for me!" Margarita threw back her head and shouted with laughter with her hands on her hips. "I'm going to make this into a game at the midway. I've got Rudy working on it. You know, whoever hits the bear with the ball can take it home. But we have to make it move out of the way just in time to make sure no one wins!" She gave me her broad smile, showing the gap between her two front teeth. "Lefèvre say that bear cost a hundred dollars."

"So I can't sell it in the ring?"

"No, no, you do it! But be sure you get a hundred dollars. Is special collectible bear only for the Reyes Bros. Ragtime Gypsy Show." Margarita tied the large bear into a basket on top of a short pole and showed me how to walk while balancing the bottom end of the pole in the palm of my hand. I could make my final round and give a little performance of my own while the cast lined up for the final circus parade curtain call.

"Practice," Margarita said, jiggling the pole and pretending to lose her balance with clumsy steps. "Make it look like a difficult trick!"

★ ★ ★

The new job gave me a chance to wear a costume in the ring as I made my rounds under the big top with furry little toy dogs, monkeys, and tigers all dangling on a T-stick I waved in the air like a baton. I tried pitching sales to the crowd in the bleachers the way I'd seen hot dog buskers do at Red Sox games back home. *Circus toys here. Only one dollar! Get your circus souvenirs!* I used a big, loud announcer's voice. I also made funny noises on a kazoo or a slide whistle; both were great sellers. I soon noticed that grandparents with small children were almost always willing to buy.

At least once a week the same grandpa edged forward and

came right down to meet me at ringside to buy the big bear in the basket, the hundred-dollar official mascot of the Reyes Bros. circus that I brought out as a single item at the end of every show. The old man wore two long braids of gray hair, and he bought the oversized bear with a single crisp bill. Sometimes he tucked his ponytail under a hat; another time he had a mustache, but I knew it was the same guy. He was reliable—always waited for me at the same spot by ring three, no matter where we'd set up the show.

With my percentage of the take in circus toy sales, I began to make more money in the ring selling toys than I had ever made in a week working with the big top crew. I enjoyed watching the acts while I walked in a tantalizingly slow fashion around all three rings. I'd pause and smile at West when he styled in front of his elephants as they reared up on hind legs. "How about *that*!" he'd crow to the crowd with an outstretched arm. The animals were so close to the spectators they could smell their dry, earthy sweat through the sawdust.

The most pungent by far were the big cats, Sheba and Sultan, who had to be brought into the ring in their cages. Five minutes in the ring with the big cats was Lefèvre's signature act, but he was careful not to perform with them when the female was in heat. The tigers could easily turn into a truly deadly pair, quick to bare their teeth and swipe with their paws. The ringmaster protected himself with a reinforced kitchen chair and kept his whip twitching at all times whenever he faced Sultan and Sheba in center ring.

The big cats performed inside an elaborate caged enclosure that looked like an enormous bird cage. It was called an arena, reminiscent of the original circus in the days of the Roman Colosseum. The ringmaster would stand erect in front of his pair of trained Bengal tigers, which were seated on pedestals. Their long tails hung down from their high perches on top of brightly painted conical drums; the tips of their tails were always in motion, lashing and spiraling in a wiry dance.

If one of the big cats—often Sheba—made a move to get down

off her pedestal, Lefèvre would snap the whip leather with a loud crack, and the wayward tiger would bare her teeth and roll her head as she returned all four paws to the seated position. Lefèvre had trained his tiger pair to jump from barrel to barrel through two hoops of fire before bounding down to the sawdust and into their cages at the edge of the ring where fresh kill—raw meat with lots of bone—was waiting for them in their feeding dishes. Circus animal handlers were quick to shut the doors, locking them up as soon as the big cats bolted toward their cages after the final trick.

"Never turn your back on a tiger," West said one evening before show time as we made our way from cage to cage in the menagerie, feeding the animals at the sideshow. Sheba and Sultan needed to eat just enough meat to keep them from attacking the ringmaster but not so much that they would want to lie down and sleep off a feast during the performance. "Tigers know exactly when to fear and when not to fear."

"Just back away?" I asked. I stood in front of the tiger cages as Sultan and Sheba scrapped for their raw meat, trapped it between their paws, and tore at the flesh. Sultan looked up from his meal with blood in his whiskers and fixed a menacing gaze on me.

"And maintain eye contact," West cautioned. "Whatever you do, don't stumble or fall down. They don't really hunt humans, but if you get too close to the ground, instinct takes over. Tigers see a crouching human as weak, and you become prey. If you encounter a tiger, stand tall, and, for God's sake, don't run."

West was teaching me all about the big circus animals, and I loved him for it. I learned how to throw a supermarket steak to one of Lefèvre's tigers by chucking it into a pullout drawer at the bottom of the cage. I had to be quick about it. The giant paw would come down and snatch the tossed meat before West had a chance to close the hatch. Claws flew through the air followed by a contented growl. At feeding time, West bowed to the power of the big cats, and he approached them naked from the waist up. I thought he was trying to keep the bloody meat juices from staining his costume shirts (one black, the other purple), but when I asked him if that was true, he told me no.

He explained: in the wild, man is always armed; in the ring, the whip only goes so far. "Big cats are intelligent; they know when they are respected and when they are loved. When they are in their cage, I take my shirt off to show them there's no weapon hidden in my clothes—no whip, nothing. Then they know it's time to eat in peace. Cats appreciate that. Tigers are always on the lookout while they feed."

Later we watched the male and female tiger pace back and forth in their cage together. Lefèvre was going to allow them to mate this summer, but the female had not yet gone into heat. Even so, as they zigzagged past one another in a circular path, the male would gently place his front paw on the female's hindquarters every so often without breaking his stride. No claws, just a bit of pressure, then more pacing and a testy growl. The female, ever elusive, ignored him and switched her tail in irritation. West looked at me and smiled.

In that moment, I sensed we were falling in love, not just acting as if we were by riding together and sharing a bunk bed. I believed then that it was real love, the kind Blacky had been talking about.

A female spider monkey with a doll's earnest expression suddenly crawled up on West's shoulder and slowly pulled a peanut out of his shirt pocket with dark wrinkled fingers. I laughed. My pleasure was absolute. This was what I had always wanted: to meet someone like West, someone who could show me a life of high adventure. West was my passport into the grand and foreign world of the circus.

★ ★ ★

After dark, I made up our bed with the new sheets I'd bought in town on my first day with the circus. I'd washed out the drawers of the old bureau that was left behind and lit the kerosene lamp. It pleased me to bring order out of the chaos of West's rumpled circus life. I wanted to create a place of peace for the two of us, an oasis we could climb into after the show was over, when we were reunited after a long day on a hardscrabble lot.

Hearing West's footsteps approaching after the evening show, I quickly took off my blouse and turned down the flame. We were alone again, chest to chest—no weapons, no clothes—nothing but voices and skin and laughter in the summer night.

It was over too soon. "Could you back up just a little, sweet Sarah?" Semen spilled in a pool between my legs, and I immediately felt sorry that we couldn't lie together for a while. "I can't believe it," West remarked. "You want to make love even when I come in after feeding the big cats. Hate to tell you, but they're waiting for me to take the elephants to teardown." I bundled myself up in a sheet and turned to the wall.

"No tears now," West put his hand on my shoulder and rocked me gently. "That happens after making love. We meet, we separate. Sometimes you laugh; sometimes you cry. You'll get used to it." He pulled the jumpsuit over his naked body and zipped it up.

"Sometimes it's hard to be apart," I said, giving him a dark look over my shoulder.

West leaned into the lower bunk where I lay and brought his soft lips to my ear, and he whispered, "Then don't you ever go." His eyes were serious as his face pulled away from mine.

The circus boy stood up at once, opened the metal door wide, and leaped into the darkness, bypassing the ladder and dropping to the ground. I could hear his footsteps in the grass as he ran off.

ON THE ROAD

7

lmost a month had passed since I'd joined the circus. We had traveled from Pennsylvania to West Virginia, looped over to Ohio, and now the circus was headed south for our scheduled dates in Kentucky and Tennessee. On the first night in Somerset, Kentucky, we'd all gotten to bed late because there was talk of a rumble, and the roustabouts had laid in wait, bracing for a fight.

"What is the fight all about? I don't get it," I asked West as we made our way back to our truck.

"In towns like this, there are always a bunch of drunks who get a charge out of beating up muscular men in makeup and tights. It's the same crowd of yahoos that picks on hippies and foreigners. Bunch of idiots," explained West.

"But everyone loves the circus; they can't wait to line up and see the show. It doesn't seem right to me." I pressed for more information. "Should I be worried?"

"Nah, forget it. It has more to do with the sex appeal of circus people than anything else. Most of the people in the hills have never seen foreigners before, much less in costume. Some rednecks feel threatened when they see a handsome man like Billy Gunga handling snakes or Lefèvre staring down a couple of tigers with his whip and those shiny black boots. They think we'll make their women lose their heads. Look at you. You ran away with me, didn't you?"

"Oh shut up!" I laughed.

The circus was completely unprotected in those days; our encampment didn't have any fencing surrounding it, and anyone could walk onto the lot unannounced at any time of day or night. I knew the circus could attract some strange people, but I thought most everyone was drawn to its magical appeal.

West and I had crawled up into the cab of our truck where we could watch what was going on. Our painted circus trucks were all lined up in their designated positions on either side of the midway, forming a kind of brightly colored avenue of primitive circus murals. The grandstand and banners for the sideshow and midway had all been packed away for the jump the next morning.

We cracked the windows and huddled together as we watched figures moving in the darkness in the open grassy corridor of the midway.

"Who are those people?" I whispered to West.

"Bootleggers. They're probably trying to sell some moonshine to the roustabouts. There are a lot of illegal stills in the hills around here."

I was relieved. At least they hadn't come to beat up the young roustabouts with long hair. Draft dodgers and war protesters weren't welcome in these parts at all, and I was especially worried about Dave and another new boy with curly hair down to his shoulders who had just joined up. For a second, I thought I saw Shorty chewing on his little stub of a cigarette on his way to join the bootleggers. As swiftly as they had come, Shorty and the bootleggers were lost from view as they disappeared into the trees.

An hour later, police cars began buzzing around the periphery of the lot, and a few officers got out, flashing their spotlights around the grounds. "Better not smoke any weed for a while," said West, putting an unlit joint back inside the brim of his circus baseball cap.

After a while, the lot fell silent, and West and I turned in, sleeping separately now that the air was so hot and sticky. He slept in the upper bunk this time, but we took turns each night because the top bunk was hotter and less comfortable. If West had to cover a long distance the next morning, I always offered him the bottom bunk. But he didn't always take it. Sleep was something we'd have paid a full day's wages for—we were so short of it.

Suddenly, in the middle of the night, we heard a man's voice screaming in the midway. Racing to open the sleeper door, we saw Shorty, on his knees, calling up to the moon, begging for mercy at the top of his lungs.

"Sweet Jesus, don't let them take me away. Aliens! Aliens is coming!" The doubled-up figure of Shorty kneeling in the dirt became a trembling mass as he shrieked, "Oh my God, there are too *many* of them! They're landing, they coming for me!"

"Shut your pie hole, and come over here, you dumbass puke!" We recognized Deuce's voice in the darkness. He staggered around as drunk as Shorty. They jostled and half wrestled each other over to Deuce's truck, and the lot settled down again.

★ ★ ★

Bang, bang, bang, bang, bang. One of the roustabouts hammered an iron stake against the metal door of our sleeper trailer. It was our five o'clock wakeup call, but the roustabout whose job it was to rouse the crew out of bed didn't bother to use his voice. He knew it would be useless to shout himself hoarse through the metal door; we were all dead to the world.

Bleary-eyed and moving slowly, West and I slid stiffly into the truck cab with dream cobwebs cluttering our minds. All over the lot, the rumble of engines turning over broke the stillness of a morning full of birdsong and ground fog. Once out on the road, I marveled at the fields we passed. I had never seen Kentucky bluegrass before. To me, it looked thick and grayish-blue, like a desert plant. I stared at it in a stupor.

"You got to talk to me. Sing, anything," West murmured. He was dog tired, I could tell.

Our first week on the road together in Pennsylvania, everything had seemed so wonderful. We were giddy, even on the earliest of summer mornings. The sun had seemed to rise just for us at the end of the highway, illuminating a new day and the beginning of a new love. Now, I began to face the serious business of making the big jumps from lot to lot as we traveled through the Appalachian Mountains. The quiet yellow lines of the highway that skimmed by mile after mile called like sirens, lulling the circus truck drivers to sleep. I had to watch West carefully because he could fall asleep, as if in a trance, with his head erect and eyes wide open, hands still gripping the steering wheel.

When we got good reception, even the radio, with its comfortable buzz and endless prattle, could lure us both into nodding off. I had to speak to stay awake myself. Once his head bobbed, West would snap it up with a jerk shouting, "No!" Talking and singing were all we had against a truck wreck.

So many laws were being broken by our convoy of painted circus trucks that Rick, our route man, had to set our course through back roads where we were least likely to be stopped or inspected by police for weight violations, unlicensed truck drivers, minors without insurance, and the various fugitives from the law who used the circus as cover until they hustled out of state.

Rick, a clean-cut, good-looking guy in a polo shirt, was not only the route man; he was Brigitte Lefèvre's boyfriend. He would leave one evening ahead of us to post the entire route with white cardboard placards printed with red arrows, which he staple-gunned onto phone poles and taped to stop signs.

Brigitte never traveled with him; the ringmaster wouldn't allow it. At twenty-two, Brigitte didn't care for performing, though she was certainly a beauty with Jackie O chestnut hair and a sweet smile. She had one of the cleanest jobs in the circus: handling the bookkeeping in the office truck.

Because the circus traveled to a new location every day, Rick had to leave for the next lot after dinner with his staple gun and red arrow placards to post the circuitous route we were to take the following morning. Sometimes the task took him all night to complete. Circus life being what it was I guessed that Lefèvre had given his daughter's lover a job that kept them apart every night on purpose. I never even saw Brigitte and Rick holding hands that entire summer.

I wondered if Lefèvre was extra strict because his wife wasn't there to keep an eye on his girls. "What about their mother?" I asked West as we drove along. "Why isn't she traveling with the show if he's so concerned about his daughters?"

"Oh Lordy. Best not bring up *that* touchy subject." West went on to explain that the ringmaster's wife had run off with another performer when Celeste was only a baby. "I'm told she was really something. She trained liberty horses and had them do all kinds of wonderful tricks, like walk across the ring on their hind legs. Then she met an acrobat—a trick rider who could trace his roots all the way back to Genghis Khan. They fell in love so hard she just up and left the country with him and left her oldest daughter, Brigitte, to bring up the little one, Celeste."

"So that's why the Reyes Bros. circus doesn't have a horse act," I concluded.

"Yeah, that's amazing when you think about it. It's the first animal act ever showcased by the circus from its beginnings over two hundred years ago. Trick riding and liberty horses will never be a part of our circus though. The ringmaster has trained his tigers to kill them."

"Jesus!"

"Yeah, Lefèvre took it that bad, according to Red," said West.

"Circus divorce," I said, without much humor.

"Yeah." Something caught in his throat when he said it. West's face looked washed out and tired. I turned my eyes back to the road.

"My mother says that when a marriage breaks up, it's usually about sex or money," I offered, trying to sound worldly.

The circus boy was silent, mulling it over. "I suppose that's it—of a fashion. I was going to say she left out *jail* and *alcohol*, but it comes down to the same thing: money." He took another pull on his cigarette, "And the stuff you end up doing when you can't get it."

"Your dad drink?" I asked.

"Oh yeah. How about yours?" West glanced over at me quickly.

"Every day, before dinner," I said.

"That's different. I'll bet he didn't knock you around."

"Jesus! No, not at all. If anything, it made him fall asleep."

We had come to a traffic light, and the truck idled noisily. West leaned over, picked up my hand, and placed it on the crown of his head. Just off-center, I felt a deep crease in his scalp, like a crevice. His dark hair was so thick the indentation had always been hidden.

"Feel that?" he asked, tipping his head my way as he handled the gearshift.

"What happened?" I traced the contours of the deep crease with my fingertips.

"Cast iron skillet."

"God!" I whispered, gently smoothing his hair back in place.

"He was okay when he was sober, but drunk, my daddy was a madman."

"You're lucky he didn't drive *you* crazy."

"Heh," West gave a short laugh. "Well, he *almost* did. Anyway, I decided not to drink—ever. I just stick to weed."

"Me too. I don't get why people drink anyway. It tastes like shit."

★ ★ ★

I remained on the lookout for the thick red arrows the route man had posted. Single red arrows indicated the direction to take along the road at critical points. Double red arrows were for turns. And one big triple arrow heralded our final turn into the lot. Missing an arrow could take us miles out of our way. Even if some of the distances didn't seem like much on paper, the poor roads and tight switchbacks stretched the length of the journey, sometimes adding on hours to a trip. The longer and more difficult the jump, the earlier we would have to get up and be on the road in the morning.

Hauling the elephants through the mountains was no easy ride either. Each pachyderm weighed four tons, and if one of them got restless en route, the trailer would fishtail perilously. This particular jump was more treacherous than usual, as we were trying to avoid a series of weigh stations. The route man knew that the elephant truck especially would never make it through.

Red had driven the elephant truck for years and had all kinds of tricks. About two hours into the jump, we saw the old man standing alone in the shadow of an ash grove, waving us down with a red bandana by the side of the road.

"Why are we stopping? What's the matter?" I turned to West who promptly downshifted and brought the rig to a standstill on the dusty shoulder of an embankment. The old man waited patiently nearby. He pulled off his baseball cap, smoothed a few wisps of white hair, and then slapped the cap against his leg before setting it squarely back on his head.

"Morning, Red." West sauntered over to the circus elder, and I followed behind. The truck engine was still rattling, choking on dirty fuel.

Red came out into the open, put his hands on his hips, and squinted at us as sunlight hit his weathered face. "Weigh station, 'bout a quarter mile up ahead. You got to take them elephants out before we can drive on through."

West turned back to the elephant truck without a word and readied the ramp by the container door for the elephants to make their descent. At that early hour, we were alone on the road, and no one was around to notice a pair of Indian elephants excitedly approaching the wilderness beyond the shallow embankment. West went over to the elephants with two long, loose foot chains. He secured one end of each chain around each elephant's front right foot and secured the other ends to trees with fat trunks. Bessie and Mary began tearing leaves and branches from the treetops, foraging for food with their trunks.

"You good to drive my truck, Red?" West called to the old man over his shoulder.

"What the hell; it's only a quarter mile on the flat. I can do that with my bum leg all right. Just get little missy to follow you on an elephant. But wait for a sign. I'll pull the horn once for all clear and three times if I need help distracting the weigh station personnel." Red peered at me from beneath his baseball cap. "You ready to ride an elephant, little lady?"

"What?" I looked at the two circus men, perplexed.

"Oh come on, Red," interrupted West. "You can't be serious."

Red threw his head back in mock surprise, knocking his own cap askew. "Oh hell, West! Haven't you taught Sarah how to ride an elephant?"

"Christ Almighty, Red. How's this going to work? You're telling me we're going to ride the elephants past a weigh station?"

I could see that West was beginning to smile. His dark eyes glinted, and I could tell he was getting excited about the possibility of outwitting the clerks.

Red leaned forward and lowered his voice to a whisper. "You got to know people, West. Them meter readers are always looking down at their numbers, and this time, they'll miss the whole show!" The old man punched his own thigh and laughed out loud. "The greatest show on earth!"

That was how I came to ride an elephant by myself: to help West get us through the weigh stations in the South. That first time I rode on Bessie's back by myself was the best though. West lifted me onto the curve of her trunk, and, as I balanced there, the elephant raised me up slowly, the wide expanse of her dome coming up into view. I grabbed on to the thick leather straps on her head harness and crawled on my hands and knees over the broad mound of her Indian-elephant forehead. Then I managed to get myself turned around on her hairy back to straddle her thick neck, tucking the folds of my long peasant skirt under my seat.

The circus boy called up to me from the ground. He looked so far away. "Just squeeze with your legs and talk to her in a deep voice," he instructed. "Pretend you're a man. Take a big breath and push all the air out of your diaphragm when you give her commands. Belt it out. When you want her to go forward, you say, 'Move up.' Just follow my lead. I'll be right in front of you."

"What do I do if she takes off? How do I get her to stop?"

"Hah, well, I don't know what to tell you," West hopped up on Mary in two easy jumps, from her bent knee to her back. "I'll yell at her myself if she does that!" he laughed to himself.

West rode ahead of me on Mary, the dominant female of the pair, and Bessie followed her, affectionately holding on to Mary's tail with her trunk. Both animals were calm and satisfied after their long chance to feed in the wild. Once the weigh station came into view over the rise in the road, we paused to watch Red's interactions with the clerks from a safe distance. At one point, we lost sight of him as he climbed back up into the cab of the empty elephant truck. There was one roly-poly man in uniform standing outside in front of a big glass picture window with a clipboard in his hand. He was waving the elephant truck past the weigh station scale with large scooping motions. The elephant truck was safely through, but it looked as if Red had to keep on driving to make room for the other trucks behind him in line. I realized that he must have been instructed to pull out of the station and get back on the highway. We heard three loud blasts from his truck horn— the call for reinforcements. West had me get off Bessie so that I could approach the clerks at the weigh station on foot.

"What do I tell them? I stared at West, wide-eyed. They're

going to think I'm a hitchhiker—or worse—if I walk in there alone."

"I don't know. Why don't you tell them that you're waiting all the way back at the end of the line, and you need to use the ladies room?"

"Yeah, all right," I agreed.

"But you need to get their attention for a while to give me enough time to walk the elephants through. Try to hustle some free coffee in exchange for a palm reading or something."

"Jesus, West," I grinned and rolled my eyes. "What next?"

"Hey, don't bullshit me. I know you can do this. Besides, you look the part."

It was true; I did look the part. I wore a long flared skirt embroidered with moons and stars and a silk scarf trimmed with fake gold coins over my head, covering my long hair. I looked like a gypsy fortuneteller.

The chubby clerk standing outside rubbed his large belly as he saw me approach. I entered the station office through a side door; only his eyes followed me inside. The office was currently empty. The chill of blasting air conditioning seized at my skin, giving me gooseflesh; the smell of stale air made gave me feel uncomfortable and claustrophobic. As the glass door closed behind me, I realized how changed I had become after living in the open for weeks. I wanted to get out of there immediately, to flee the hum of machines, the blinking fluorescent lights, and the metallic patter coming from the fuzzy black-and-white TV no one was watching.

Looking out through a large picture window, I saw one of our heavy circus trucks drive up on the scale. The pole truck was eventually waved through by the roly-poly clerk who was still stationed outside. Through the picture window, I made eye contact with the driver, Shorty, who acknowledged my look imperceptibly by lifting his chin and scratching his nose. Then the roustabout fixed his eyes on the road ahead, put his truck in gear, eased his rig off the scale, and moved on.

I heard a toilet flush in a bathroom behind me, and another clerk with a badge, who looked like a supervisor, jumped slightly when he saw me waiting in the office. I smiled at him.

"Ma'am?" he tilted his chin toward me and was about to speak again when the pot-bellied clerk entered the station. Now there were two officials facing me, one on either side of me. The supervisor who had just stepped out of the bathroom was older; he was a tall, bald-headed, mean-looking man I pegged as the boss who let his grunt do all the work. At once I began to speak to the weigh station officials, using the Spanish accent and husky tone I'd picked up from Margarita.

"Gentlemen, I beg of you. One favor, one favor only," I said.

Both of them leaned in closer. I made a show of adjusting the halter top at my breastbone and sighed deeply. After I asked for a cup of coffee, I offered the pot-bellied clerk a palm reading. "Please, let me see your hand, kind sir. There is something about your future that is calling out to me, something you must know before it is too late."

The supervisor struck me as the serious type, a skeptic. Nevertheless, he hung around to watch as I trailed my index finger along the lines of the chubby clerk's palm. I made sure to stand facing the picture window so that the two men had their backs to the goings-on outside.

"Your hands are square in shape," I said, gently taking the junior clerk's left hand and then the right in my hands and examining them thoroughly, squeezing the fleshy mounts and assessing each joint. "Your joints are noticeably strong and well-developed. These are the hands of a practical person, someone able to get things done with as little chaos as possible."

"How about that!" my new client exclaimed. Color rose in his face, and he shifted his weight from one foot to the other. "What else do you see?"

I palpated the meaty flesh at the base of his thumb, "Your mount of Venus is very—"

"I got to hear this one!" the tall, bald supervisor chortled. He leaned over, hands on his narrow hips. I could smell the pasty stench of his coffee breath.

"I don't quite know how to describe the mount of Venus to a square-handed man such as yourself." I looked up flirtatiously at the hefty young clerk. "You would seem to be a man of moderation in all other respects. I would not wish to offend ..."

Both men waited for me to speak. "Your mount of Venus is quite pronounced," I declared with authority, delicately pinching the flesh.

"Yeah, I know. I got ham hocks for hands," the fat clerk said in embarrassment, drawing his hand away from me slightly. But before he could slide out of my grip, I arrested the clerk's hand and guided it back toward me and held his palm open, just under my breasts. Both men leaned over even farther. "Please don't misunderstand me," I implored. "A big, fleshy mount of Venus is a beautiful thing. It means that you are a sensual lover with a large ... an abundant ... an abundance of energy."

"Really?" scoffed the supervisor, taking a step backward and lifting his head to force out a false laugh. "Well, don't think you're getting any extra vacation time, buddy. Just so you know." I had been glancing up every so often to track West's progress in shadow on the far side of the road as he walked the elephants past the station. At one point, I even saw him run ahead of Bessie and Mary and command them to catch up to him at a trot, just as he did every evening after teardown. But controlling both elephants at once wasn't going well. Bessie had stopped to forage in the trees. West was in full view, waving a leafy branch, frantically beckoning his wayward elephant to follow him.

"What are you looking at?" asked the sardonic supervisor as I took one last surreptitious peek over the head of the pudgy man in front me. I lowered my gaze at once, zeroing in on the junior clerk's forehead. The supervisor continued on, "Are you looking into his mind? 'Cause if you are, you won't find nothing there!" He chuckled at his own joke.

"I am reading his aura," I intoned. "It contains a message of great importance. It can tell us everything."

"Can you tell me if I'm going to die?" the softer clerk was becoming more and more nervous. His palm began to perspire beneath my fingertips.

"Can't be soon enough!" snorted the bald clerk.

I ignored his attempt at comedy and assured my client in a soothing voice. "No one but God knows the hour of your death. Your aura will show you only good things: your spirit and the path your spirit wishes you to take."

"Right," sneered the unpleasant official. "Right down the hall and into the bathroom with the newspaper."

I pretended I hadn't heard and continued on, desperate to manufacture another excuse to look out the picture window to check on West. "I will search your aura more deeply to reveal its message to you," I said as I flicked my eyes all around the room, eventually capturing a glimpse through the picture window. West was gone. He and his elephants had made it through.

Feeling compassion for the rotund clerk who had entrusted his future to me, I made a bold prediction as I folded his palm into a loose fist as a sign of closure. "In the future, you will be honored for your kind heart and good deeds. You will be promoted to a position of greater authority within a year."

The supervisor didn't laugh at all this time, and the junior clerk's face lit up with a shit-eating grin that stretched from ear to ear. I left in a great hurry, leaving a half-drunk cup of coffee behind. At some distance down the road, I recognized our elephant truck by its distinctive murals of Serpentina and the fire-eater. West and Red were waiting for me inside. I swung up into the cab next to Red.

"You okay? We thought you'd never get out of there!" West leaned forward, speaking to me past Red.

"Yeah, I don't think they suspected a thing," I replied.

"How about you? Are Bessie and Mary on board?" I yelled over the engine noise as West turned the ignition and threw the truck in gear.

At the sound of their names one of the elephants trumpeted loud and long. We all burst out laughing.

"Holy shit, we'd better hit the road!" West gunned the accelerator, and we pulled out onto the highway so fast that the trailer fishtailed back and forth. I could hear Bessie and Mary banging their trunks against the container walls in protest.

"Don't jackknife the rig, you shitfaced candy ass!" Red banged both hands on the dashboard and howled with laughter. Tears came to his eyes. "We did it, goddammit! Best goddamn day of my whole goddamn life!"

With the windows down, we sang the "Hit the Road, Jack" refrain at the top of our lungs until the weigh station was several hills and several towns behind us.

★ ★ ★

We traveled for thirty miles before stopping at a roadside restaurant; we were the last circus truck to pull into the parking lot. After a difficult jump, this rest stop would be a welcome relief. I would be able to use a real bathroom instead of the putrid donniker on the lot and avoid the hideous leering of the half-wit, Donniker Dick, who tended that trailer. The stench and mountain of filth were horrendous, worse than the pig sty back on the family farm, but there was nowhere else for the roustabouts to go. I was the only female on the setup crew. After I'd used the outhouse-style donniker a few times, Donniker Dick made a hole in the wall so he could have a good view while I went.

The morning stop at a breakfast diner always gave me a chance to perform simple morning rituals in peace. Shining porcelain, soap, and hot water had become unspeakable luxuries.

Joining West at a table, I found all the roustabouts trying to outdo one another, as usual, with stories of their most recent exploits. Red was holding forth on our run past the weigh station. When I arrived, a cheer went up among the circus crew.

"What do you mean, they didn't see you?" one of the roustabouts asked West. "How you going to hide a couple of elephants?"

"Well, looks like West has got some secret weapon," Deuce chimed in. "Miss Sarah just walked in there and showed them her womanly charms, and the clerks were putty in her hands."

"Now *that's* entertainment!" Jesse hollered.

"Oh man, what the hell did she do in there?" Shorty wanted to know. He looked at me with his beady little close-set eyes and wiggled a cigarette stub around in his mouth.

"I saw it all!" Deuce called out. "The two of them weigh station clerks pretended to get their fortunes told, so they could stick their heads down her blouse!"

Oh come on, Deuce," I shot back, "Don't get any wild ideas. It was just a palm reading, something to keep them busy—"

"Oh yeah? Well, Miss Sarah, you can read my palm all day!" Deuce slapped his hand down on the table and guffawed.

"And she should read your tattoos too!" Jesse spoke up in his rich southern drawl, "The ones all up and down your fine behind!" Deuce smiled good-naturedly and allowed Jesse to take the spotlight, ceding the floor to the man from Alabama. "What about Tarzan over there?" Jesse pointed his stubbly chin in West's direction at the far corner of the table. "How the hell you make eight tons of elephant disappear?"

"It wasn't easy, but I had my partner in crime here do all the hard work." West put his arm around me, pulled me close, and kissed my cheek right in front of them. Then he leaned back, eyes downcast, and folded his hands over his ribs. For a moment, the circus boy looked thoughtful.

"But the truth of the matter is," West began, "we left some solid evidence." When he looked up, I could see a hint of merriment in his eyes. Red gasped and choked, suddenly overcome with mirth. "Yes sir," the old man agreed. "Judging from the size of the dung heaps Mary left behind, those dumbass clerks will be calling in to report 'a disturbance in the atmosphere!'" he quipped.

"Or a meteor shower!" one roustabout threw out.

"Hell! They'll be running for the hills; they'll think there's been an alien invasion!" Red hollered. He waved his cap in the air before collapsing on his elbows with laughter.

The roustabouts whooped and celebrated; some stood up and rubbed their knuckles into West's head. Others pounded him on the back.

"Hey! Martians is landing in Kentucky!" crowed Deuce. And then they told by turns the story of what had happened to Shorty the previous night in Somerset.

"Bootleggers showed up around midnight, and Shorty went off with them to their still. He got so plastered on moonshine he saw double. Maybe even triple! He thought the moon was a spaceship!" said Deuce.

Another roustabout explained that Shorty saw the full moon multiply itself and transform into a series of bright, flashing lights across the sky.

"Aliens! Aliens is coming! Oh my Jesus!" Deuce imitated a whimpering Shorty, getting down on his knees. "Yeah, and then he took off up a goddamn mountain!"

"What the hell for?" prodded Jesse.

"To commit suicide!" Deuce howled, tears of laughter in his eyes.

"Huh! That right?" Jesse swirled his last swig of coffee and gulped it down.

"I had to go get him and talk him down," said Deuce, warming to his story. "By the end of the night, he was on his knees in the middle of the midway, praying for the aliens not to take him away and screaming, 'God bless America!' Shorty's *still* not quite right in the head."

"If he ever was," Jesse remarked.

Our table was unexpectedly bathed in sunlight as the screen door opened, briefly illuminating the dark wood-paneled interior of the greasy spoon truck stop where we had gathered. I noticed that a few heads turned in Billy Gunga's direction as he entered the roadside café with his Philippine wife and infant daughter; he and his family were the only dark-skinned people in the place. I felt a ripple of hostility in the air that set my nerves on high alert. Turning my attention back to our table, I noticed the roustabouts seemed unconcerned. West ignored the performers' entrance and continued his conversation with Jesse.

"You can't mess with that moonshine stuff," said West, shaking his head.

"Damn straight!" Jesse agreed. "Hey, sister!" he called out to the waitress. "Can we get another cup of coffee for my friend here?" He tipped his head in Shorty's direction. Shorty was staring into the bottom of his empty coffee cup, as if he had found God down there.

The waitress, in a pale pink uniform, was taking the Indian magician's breakfast order at the performers' tables on the opposite side of the room where the Gungas had been seated with other foreign circus stars. She straightened her back and called over her shoulder, "Be right there, darlin'. Just give me a sweet minute to take care of these folks."

Incensed, Jesse stabbed out his morning cigarette, got up, and wandered over to the jukebox. Hands on hips, he read the titles of the selection of 45s and let out a snort. "Hey, Billy Gunga, this one is for you!" he hollered across the diner to the bank of tables where the performers had settled in with their families. Then Jesse rummaged in his pockets for change and slipped a couple of quarters in the play slot.

The music started up. After a few bars, I caught up with the lyrics: "He wasn't all coon. Maybe just a high yella," which was followed by the rousing refrain, "Some niggers never die; they just smell that way ..."

The Indian man got up without a word, gave Jesse his back as he bent over to pick up his baby daughter, and calmly ushered his wife out the door. The screen door snapped shut with a bang and a jingle.

Jesse burst out laughing. "We're in the South *now*!"

A sick feeling pulled at my stomach. The circus was not one big happy family, as I originally envisioned. The roustabouts and the performers lived in different worlds. I loved Billy Gunga and his beautiful family. He had been the first person to talk to me at the circus, the first one to invite me over to his mobile home for a dish of Indian curry he had prepared himself. His wife, Lily, gave me costume pieces and fabrics from India that I used to sew my own outfits for parading around in the ring with the circus toys. She had even taught me how to do a little styling to increase sales, how to stand up on my toes, extend a graceful arm, and smile wide "like a bally girl."

★ ★ ★

By the time our truck pulled into our spot on the new lot in La Follette, Tennessee, a crowd had already gathered around Billy Gunga. The magician was wearing a richly embroidered velvet vest and jeweled turban as he displayed a long dark serpent with a belly over four inches in diameter he'd just found in the tall grass at the edge of the lot.

"It's a blue racer," the conjurer smiled. He glowed with good health and had perfect white teeth. The black snake coiled itself around Billy's gleaming, coppery forearms.

Lefèvre's youngest daughter, Celeste, begged to practice handling the snake so that she could promote herself to stardom as Cleopatra, the snake charmer, at the sideshow. Incredibly, Celeste managed to upstage Serpentina in one day with her act, relying heavily on a cape and a shiny costume that barely covered her slender, adolescent body.

Celeste was a rail-thin thirteen-year-old grandstander with

large purple-blue eyes and uneven teeth. After learning to juggle and balance on a large ball, she sometimes got to stand in for Serpentina at the sideshow. Celeste was as tall as Serpentina, but she could not fill out her spectacular sparkling costumes.

Celeste only got to perform once as Cleopatra, the snake charmer, in the sideshow. The following day, the snake was gone. No one seemed to know where the blue racer had been caged for the night. At least not until we were all heading out in the summer heat the next day in our circus convoy onto the open highway.

I ended up riding to the next lot with Brigitte in her Mustang convertible. West had told me that he and Jesse needed to ride together. They had "things to discuss."

"What things?'

"Things that don't concern you, sugar," he'd said, and when my face fell, he tousled my hair. "Some things you're just too young to know about."

"Oh, so you'll tell me when I'm twenty-one, huh?"

"Yeah, something like that."

When we hit the highway, I lay back in the leather passenger seat in Brigitte's open convertible and enjoyed the warm wind as it snatched at my headscarf. I liked Brigitte. She was quiet and reserved; she did not flaunt her voluptuous body like the seasoned women who performed in the ring. While her younger sister, Celeste, craved attention, Brigitte avoided it, and she still turned every circus hand's head on the lot.

One hour into the jump, Brigitte, in her up-do, sunglasses, and tight pencil skirt, drove her Mustang convertible alongside the light truck until it was riding parallel with Jesse's rig. Then, digging a high heel into the floorboards, she pressed hard on the accelerator and tried to pass him on the right. Jesse responded to the competition immediately and gunned his engine, playing the fool, alternately speeding up and slowing down so that he could lean over and get a good view down Brigitte's low-cut T-shirt from his trucker's perch.

When I gave him the finger, he just pulled the cord to sound his truck horn and gave us a big blast. This game continued, with both vehicles traveling in tandem, until Brigitte gave up racing and fell behind in her convertible, allowing Jesse to speed on ahead. Noticing our absence, he slowed down immediately, and, as his truck window lined up with our open car, we heard him yell in terror, as if the brakes were failing, "Oh my *God!*"

When I turned in my seat to look up and see what the matter was, I saw the blue racer snake coiled up on the dashboard in the truck cab; its head was raised up, staring right into Jesse's face. In one hellish movement, Jesse gripped the snake's diamond-shaped head and hurled the whole length of its long, ropey body out the open truck window past West, who ducked, flattening himself on the seat. That done, Jesse hollered, "Hot damn!" and clamped his foot on the accelerator and thundered off down the road. West would tell me later that his heart didn't stop pumping hard until they reached the next lot.

What Jesse and West never saw was the erratic flight path of the black snake as it fell, landing heavily in the rear seat of Brigitte's Mustang convertible. The serpent slipped to the floor right behind me with a menacing hiss and soon made its way under the driver's seat toward Brigitte and her bare legs. There was a round of female screaming, then shrieking as Brigitte and I panicked, jumping up into our seats with our feet tucked under us at the sight of the wriggling black tail spiraling toward the gas pedal. Brigitte's car began to weave out of control until I pulled the emergency brake. Both of us ended up with our fingers wrapped around the wheel, trying desperately to pull over and come to a stop.

Seconds later, we skidded to the edge of the road. I vaulted out of the car in one giant leap without opening the passenger door. Performers in their cars and mobile homes pulled over in a hail of gravel and lined up end-to-end in the breakdown lane. Brigitte's lone convertible had been abandoned, the driver's side door left hanging open. She observed it from a distance, shifting her weight nervously in her high heels, biting a brightly-painted thumbnail.

The snake, having grown accustomed to making its nest in cars and trucks, had slithered under the seat and would not move. Finally, Billy Gunga approached the car with a long stick that had a large hook at the end. "Is there a problem?" he inquired with a hint of mock courtesy.

The Indian man was the only true snake charmer in our entourage. He opened both doors as wide as they would go and sat in the Mustang for several minutes. When the snake didn't appear, he calmly reached under the seat with his long stick, gently turning the hook so that it lifted the snake from beneath without piercing its skin. Once captured on Gunga's snake hook, the snake comforted itself by wrapping its long body in a spiral around the stick. The conjurer gave a little bow to those of us who had gathered to watch; he smiled and cocked his head at an angle so that the jeweled ornament pinned to his turban dangled off to one side. Then, standing erect, he balanced the stick holding the snake on the top of his turban and made his way over to the undergrowth at some distance from Brigitte's car. He walked along, hands free, still balancing the stick like a pole on the top of his head—arms outstretched for dramatic effect. I stood there, gawking.

Lily, his wife, leaned over and whispered to me, "He does that all the time. We have a thick metal tray hidden in the top of his turban for his balancing act."

At the edge of the woods, Gunga carefully removed the wooden snake pole from his head with both hands and touched the stick gently to the ground, like a wand. The blue racer, sensing the safety of plentiful camouflage, rapidly uncoiled and disappeared into the grass in one liquid motion. Some of us applauded Gunga's snake charmer performance by the side of the road, but Brigitte was not amused. For the rest of the summer, the ringmaster's eldest daughter traveled in an air-conditioned mobile camper. I never saw her drive her Mustang convertible again with the windows down, radio blasting—not even with her boyfriend, the route man.

WATER BOY

8

noticed that Lefèvre and his daughters, Rick, and the rest of the performers all lived in their own mobile homes. In short order, I learned about the circus hierarchy. It all had to do with who got water first once we got to the lot. A strange young man named Wayne drove the water truck; he had pale skin and even paler wispy hair and glasses. I had seen him for the first time in a darkened phone booth the night I arrived at the circus by bus in Bloomsburg, Pennsylvania. I'd recognized him by his ragged cut-off shorts and how he wore shoes without socks. None of the other men at the circus, performers or roustabouts, went around in short shorts and bare ankles. I still wondered why he had called himself Superman on the phone. I smiled to myself. Did he plan— like Clark Kent—to change his clothes in that phone booth?

Wayne's first destination every morning was the local fire station. There he would fill the large water tank on the back of a stake truck before driving onto the lot. In small towns, the fire station and police station were either located side by side or were housed in the same building. Whenever people needed to know where to find the show, they could call the local police who always knew where we had set up camp.

The water boy had a strict routine once he'd checked in with the fire station in the morning. If the animal trucks were in,

Wayne would help West fill oil drums with water for the elephants and then make his way to the menagerie to provide water for the big cats and monkeys.

West always managed to get into conversation with the water boy whenever he came by in the morning. Bessie and Mary each needed an entire oil drum full of water to last the day, and they took a while to fill.

One morning while I was sweeping out our sleeper trailer, I overheard West arguing with the water boy. "*When* then? For Christ's sake, Wayne!" West growled as he coiled up the hose that had been used to fill both drums.

"How the hell should I know?" the water boy snapped back, his voice high and tight. Then he hopped up into the water truck and turned the ignition. "I got other things to deal with."

"I bet you do," West called up to him over the noise of the engine. "You better watch yourself!" It was a threat—I had no doubt in my mind. I wondered what was up with those two, but I decided to keep my questions to myself for the time being. West seemed to be itching for a fight; I'd learned not to dig too deep when he was all riled up.

All during setup, the water boy could be found hooking up his truck to each mobile home, pumping in water. Finally, when the tent was set up, the roustabouts lined up by their trucks with buckets to fill for bathing. T-shirts were left hanging from open cab doors, and some men shaved in the rear-view mirrors. It occurred to me that in the circus, the elephants were at the top of the pyramid, along with the menagerie animals; next in the hierarchy came the performers and finally, the circus crew—us—the lowly roustabouts.

There was a spigot on the side of the water truck, and while everyone was napping in the hot afternoon after lunch, I liked to wash my long hair all alone under the rush of cold water—after everyone else had taken their share of water. The water ran down the front of my halter top, but I didn't care; it was such a wonderful feeling to lather shampoo under the icy water. I would stay bent over with soap in my eyes for a good while. That afternoon, while I was luxuriating under the spigot, I heard a couple of roustabouts speaking in low voices in the truck cab of the water truck.

"Alabama! Are you crazy? Don't you know I got a whole lot of history there?"

I recognized Jesse's voice. Quickly, I dried myself off and tied my wet hair up in a terry towel turban, but not before I heard Wayne reply to Jesse, "You want Lefèvre to red-light you? We can make that happen too, you know. The deal goes down—double this time—whether you do it or West does it. Just thought you might like a bigger cut."

I turned off the tap, and the water tank gurgled and went silent.

"Hold on." Jesse had heard me. The slim roustabout from Alabama with the jelly roll haircut emerged from the truck cab and stepped toward me with a smile. He looked me up and down with his arms folded across his chest. Then spying my stiff nipples and the curve of my breasts beneath the water-soaked halter top, he clapped his hands, bent over, and then put his hands on his knees. He beckoned to me as if I were a golden retriever puppy. "Hoo-whee, what do we have here? Miss All Sweetness and Light? Getting ready to go play stink finger with your low-life boyfriend?"

"Mind your own business." I glowered at him and backed away, hurriedly pulling the terry towel from my head and wrapping it around my chest.

"Hey!" Jesse shouted and turned back to Wayne, who was now hanging one-handed out of the truck cab, taking a look at what was causing the commotion. "That's *my* line. MYO—god-damn—B!" He chuckled to himself and sauntered off, hips loose in his jeans, shaking his head. He ran his fingers through the wide front curl of his jelly roll and smoothed his hair back.

The next time I was with West alone in the sleeper, I confronted him. "I need to know what's going on with you and Jesse and Wayne. Are you guys dealing drugs or something?"

West didn't react with surprise, but he got up and closed the sleeper door. When he turned to respond, he looked weary. "Welcome to the circus. Like I told you, there's a little bit of sketchy business going on, but it only lasts while we run through the Kentucky/Tennessee corridor. We got some marijuana farmers who need us to make a delivery farther south, that's all."

"In Alabama?"

"Hey, now why would I want to get you all mixed up in this? The less you know the better off you'll be. Anyway, it's on Jesse this time. I'm out of it." The circus boy fished for his cigarettes in his shirt pocket and shook one out of the pack.

"Jesse seemed real uptight about making a drop in Alabama."

"Yeah, well, I guess he's got his reasons, like everybody else."

"Aren't *you* worried?" I began to observe West's movements in the mirror from my seated position at the edge of the bunk bed. His shoulders were tightening almost imperceptibly.

"Tennessee hillbillies have been making money off of moonshine in the backwoods for years." The circus boy leaned into his cupped hand and lit one up. After taking a smooth drag, his body relaxed; he had completed the rituals he required to spin a story. "They got a whole apparatus for running illegal substances. Now that Prohibition days are over, the next generation is growing pot. Same difference. They got a right to make a living. I don't mind helping out." He sat down next to me and rested his elbows on his knees.

"You're a drug smuggler," I said.

"Yeah," West gave a short laugh, "you could say that, but that's not *all* I am. I'm a draft dodger and a bastard with nowhere to turn. Lefèvre holds all the cards in this operation. I'm just an employee. If he wants me to shovel shit, I shovel shit. If he wants me to run a little marijuana, I make drops along the road. Either way, I'm making money."

"You get paid for this?"

"Sure. And so do you." He tapped the ash on the wooden floor and smudged it with his work boot.

"Wait a minute …"

"Don't play dumb." West looked up at me and cocked his head to one side. "You really think some old geezer is so crazy about you he'll follow you and pony up a Benjamin for an oversized teddy bear every week?"

"You made *me* a part of this?"

"Had to. How else was I going to convince Lefèvre to let you stay?"

I stared at him, openmouthed.

"I'm just trying to make my way out of this mess best I can," he continued. "You wouldn't understand. You've got a family to run home to." I started to protest, but he interrupted me. "Fact is I should have put you on a bus back home a long time ago. I knew you were jailbait too." West looked at me hard and then shook his head slowly from side to side. "I just couldn't do it. You got under my skin."

We fell silent as I thought things over. I got up and opened the sleeper door to let in a fresh breeze. I stayed there leaning against the door sill, staring out at the elephants as they tossed clouds of dirt up on their backs with their trunks.

"So," West stood up and joined me by the door. He chucked his spent filter out on the ground, and then he wrapped his arms around my waist from behind and propped his chin on my shoulder. "Are you in or out?"

"I'm not going anywhere," I said. "I love everything about the circus: our life on the road, the crazy people we meet, the animals, the performers. It's what I want out of life—to have something happening all the time." I turned to face him. "Even if it's hard sometimes, here I'm more alive every minute of the day than I ever was at home."

West's whole face melted into a peaceful smile that told me we had cleared another hurdle; we were one step closer to an intimacy neither of us had experienced before. "It's not all sweetness and light, sugar. You got to get your hands dirty—maybe a little dirtier than you anticipated. Just pretend you don't know a thing, and keep it that way."

"And if I don't?" I teased.

West's hands wandered from my waist to my hips, and he pulled me to him roughly. "I'll spank you. Is that what you want?"

Somehow the threat of a little danger just added to my daily ration of circus excitement. I grinned with all my teeth at West and playfully pushed him away with both hands on his chest. "Spank *me*? No way! Who likes that?"

"Some folks do. People are weirder than animals," West chuckled.

I recalled overhearing my name mentioned in a conversation among the candy butchers at the cookhouse and something about "making love filthy." I mentioned the conversation to West. "Do you know what they were talking about?" I asked.

West took my hand. "Listen, Sarah. There are a thousand ways to make love. It doesn't matter if you lie down in a nice big bed in a private mobile home or in the back of an elephant truck. What we've got nobody is going to take away."

★ ★ ★

Now that I was selling toys in the ring every day, I spent my mornings stringing together and mending toys at Margarita's camper over at the performers' row while West was busy with the elephants, putting up the tent with the crew. Margarita's boyfriend, Rudy Holiday, asked me to make some pencil drawings of his plans for a petting zoo; he wanted to pitch it as a new attraction. While making sketches of farm animals in a webbed folding chair outside Margarita's camper, I became a familiar face, a fixture in the makeshift neighborhood, always talking to the other performers about their lives and how they came to join the circus.

Seventy-two-year-old Fritz had spent his entire life performing as an acrobat, aerialist, juggler, and clown; he was the oldest performer on the lot. He had only recently recovered from extensive surgery on his arms, damaged from decades of catching his brother in the air. Soon after the operation, he returned to the circus to work up less physically demanding new acts as a clown—a Western comedy and a dog act.

"How are you able to do all that slapstick stuff when you reenact the bar fight in your Western act?" I asked him one day. I was amazed at how agile he appeared in makeup and his zoot suit clown costume when he performed in the ring with his son. I had assumed both men were about the same age.

"A little pain doesn't matter for a performer; we're not soft. I come from a circus family in Germany. My parents and my grandparents all performed under the big top. My mother was an acrobat on horseback, and my father was a clown. I began traveling the circus route a few months after I was born."

"Did you get to perform with your parents?"

"As a small boy, I did an acrobatics act with my brother and sister. I performed as a girl until I was fourteen. Then I didn't look like a girl anymore."

I looked at his expressive clown's face; he had wrinkles around his eyes and mouth, and his thick hair was brushed back off his forehead. His features were perfectly even, and his eyes were kind. *He must have been a very handsome young man*, I thought.

"Do you miss performing in Europe?"

"Yes, it was wonderful," the aging clown reminisced. "There were bright lights, and all four sides had big bands playing." The old circus performer gestured vigorously with his arms like a conductor, keeping time with an imaginary baton in his right hand. He raised his voice. "And everybody was always in uniform."

I knelt down to stroke the ruff of one of his six trained white Eskimo dogs. "How long does it take to train a dog like this?" I asked as the Spitz cast a watchful eye at its master.

"It depends on the dog. They are like people. Some are very interested and learn in one year. Some could take seventy-two years, and they would still not be ready."

We smiled as Fritz lifted the jaw of his lead dog, looked into its canine eyes, and spoke lovingly to his performing animal, "Is that not so? Yes?"

"Do you think you'll ever stop traveling?"

"I want to work with the circus as long as I can," he said, and then he added with a sober face, "and if I ever have to quit—damn it—I'd rather die."

Being around the performers changed my status at the circus. They knew I was there to stay, and I began to make the transition from townie to circus girl.

There were a few odd jobs circus employees could do for extra pay. Most were accomplished after setup was completed, when all the other roustabouts were catching up on their sleep—sacked out under their trucks after lunch. One of the roustabouts taught me how to "rope the blues," the wooden boards painted blue for grandstand bleacher seating. Even old man Red let me take over his spot as ticket taker at the sideshow. Eventually Lefèvre relented and started giving me a regular paycheck again.

"Where you been, second love?" Red hailed me from his folding chair outside the office truck as I ambled over to the sideshow entrance.

"I been sacking out!" I wisecracked.

"Ha! We'll make a circus bum out of you yet! I see you're getting a lot of cherry pie these days," he said, raising his furry eyebrows and whistling softly. "You deserve it. Your face is a lot prettier than mine," he crowed. "I probably just scare all them townies away! Besides, now you know how to keep people from teasing the elephants."

Traveling every day became routine, and I could tell the time by the music that accompanied each circus act. I was no longer a "trailer," someone who followed the show without a paycheck; I had become a trouper, someone on the circus payroll who signed on and stayed for the whole season.

★ ★ ★

At the start of the traditional school year in September, a group of acrobats and jugglers asked me to tutor their children under the big top when it was quiet between shows. Circus children, like their parents, would stay with the show until it ended in October, but then they would have to integrate into a local school system a month late—an awkward adjustment after five months on the road.

I started meeting the Palmieri acrobat children every afternoon on the bleachers under the big top. They'd bend over their dog-eared workbooks and scribble away dutifully.

The Palmieri acrobat children were mature for their years. The oldest, Alessandro, a beautiful eleven-year-old boy with tan skin and blond hair that fell to his chin, carried the family mantle. The younger two, Chiara and Silvana, aged ten and nine, were charming little girls with curly hair and sweet faces. Like most circus families, they performed in two or three acts that involved different family members. The husband and wife were flyers, and they performed their aerial act with catches and somersaults. The children, headlined by Alessandro, performed a tumbling act that culminated in a show of strength as the father joined his family at the end and balanced his wife and all three children on his shoulders in a human tower. The husband and wife were regal masters of their craft; grace radiated from their fingertips as they drew applause for every successful trick with arms that flew up in the air.

The boy, Alessandro, stunned crowds with his beauty and his powerful series of back-flips across the ring. I marveled at his talent—he was always practicing on a tightrope setup outside his family camper, but I also feared for him. Sometimes people gathered to watch him there. Wayne, the water boy, would linger by the Palmieri camper with his shirt off. And I had seen him there in an attitude of morbid fascination more than once. Was he really just going about his business, filling up the water tanks in the performers' mobile homes? Once I even photographed him leaning against the camper watching Alessandro, the young prince, step across the wire in ballet slippers.

I learned more about the Palmieri family when I met them at their trailer to take the children to "school" under the big top. Mr. Palmieri wanted me to teach his children on the weekdays, just as if they were attending regular classes.

"We started off as the Palmieri Babies," explained ten-year-old Chiara, "but then we got too old!" she giggled. "Now we're the Palmieri Kids!"

"So you have always performed? All your life?" I asked.

"Always. I don't remember not performing," chirped Silvana, the youngest of the three.

Alessandro sprang onto the stretched-out tightwire that was eight inches off the ground and began to walk across it, balancing easily without a pole. Then he picked up speed, sliding the soft leather soles of his ballet slippers for traction, before leaping backward to execute a backflip and nailing the landing on the wire again.

"We want to be wire walkers when we grow up," Chiara said, tilting her chin in the direction of her brother.

"And trapezists—like Mom and Dad," boasted Silvana.

"Yeah, like Dick Grayson's mom and dad," added Alessandro, jumping off to lift his sister into the air. Their movements were automatic, punctuated by simple one-syllable commands.

"Hep!" Alessandro commanded, and Silvana, who had already placed her foot on Alessandro's knee, jumped up into his arms.

He pressed her over his head as his sister extended her arms and legs in a perfect horizontal plane. I applauded lightly and urged them to get ready for school.

Eventually, the Palmieri children were allowed to walk un-accompanied across the lot over to the main tent, carrying their workbooks and pencil cases. During the quiet hours between shows, the big top was a pleasant place to work. The afternoon sun shining through the tent canvas cast an amber glow on the interior. With tent flaps open at the front and back, cool breezes flowed through the cavernous space. There were no crowds, no smells of cotton candy and popcorn, and no chaotic grandstand speeches and tinny music blasting through the PA system. Just red and white ring curbs arranged on the ground in three giant circles and the aerial equipment hanging in place. Props baskets lined the performers' entrance corridor. Everything about the big top at rest spoke of the show that was to come.

On most days, we sat high up in the bleachers. The acrobat children were so flexible that they liked to sit straddle, placing their workbooks in front of them on the seating. They rested their chins on one fist, lazily filling in their answers with a pencil stub.

"I hate school," said Alessandro flatly, lifting his head from his work.

"Why?" I asked, knowing full well I would get nowhere if I disagreed.

"I have to take ballet class every day when I'm not perform-ing," the acrobat boy said softly.

"They tease him! He's the only boy in ballet class with us!" chirped his little sister, Chiara. She giggled, and her delicate curls bounced around her heart-shaped face.

Alessandro clammed up and scowled.

"That must be really tough," I said.

"I hate it." The eleven-year-old acrobat corrected himself quickly, "Not the ballet, the teasing. I have to do the ballet. My father would kill me if I quit."

"I bet you wish you could make the bullies shut up," I offered.

"My father went through the same thing. He told me I will become very strong if I continue. Then no one will bother any of us," he paused and began flipping through a *Batman* comic book he had tucked into the center of his workbook. Without looking at me, he said, "I promised to protect my sisters when he dies."

"Where did you get that?" I asked, pointing to the comic book. The Palmieri children never left the lot by themselves. Mr. Palmieri was a strict father. I knew that candy and comic books were off limits. I held out my hand, and the acrobat boy handed over the comic book.

"Wow," I said, glancing at the cover. "It's the issue where Robin and Superman team up!" My young boy cousins had been wild to buy this issue when it came out.

"Don't tell, please," Alessandro pleaded. "I like to read, really. I just don't like to read stuff for school."

"I don't mind if you read it," I said, handing the *Detective Comics* book back to Alessandro, "but I don't want your father to think *I* gave it to you."

I decided to give a surprise spelling test to bring the class back to task. The Palmieri children snapped to attention and stared at me. "This should be an easy word for you," I said, making eye contact with all three of them. "Circus," I dictated.

In unison, the young acrobats bent their heads over their workbooks and began to scribble out the word. I waited, spying spelling mistakes in their workbooks: "sirkis," "surcuss," "syrcus."

"Okay, Alessandro," I smiled. "Go outside and see if that's right. It's painted on the marquee tent at the entrance: *Welcome to the circus.*

Happy to be free to move about, Alessandro scampered off, cartwheeling his way across the empty performance rings without even looking back to see who was watching. I continued dictating a few more words and then moved on to arithmetic problems, checking the girls' work and wondering why Alessandro had not yet returned. Exasperated, I left the Palmieri sisters and went off in search of their brother, but he was nowhere in view as I exited the big top.

How dare he walk out on me like that? I thought. Now I was thoroughly irritated, and I resolved to wrap up the tutoring session and walk the girls back to their family camper. I was already imagining a furious Mr. Palmieri. Their life was one of rock-solid discipline, precision, and control.

Suddenly a fight broke out somewhere on the far side of the lot. Men's voices could be heard, yelling at each other, and truck doors were banging. In confusion, I quickly ushered the girls toward their mobile home as six white Eskimo dogs burst through the midway at a full run. The German animal trainer followed his dogs swiftly on his wiry legs, giving commands in sharp bursts with the precision of a drill sergeant. From a distance, we heard Mr. Palmieri yell in Italian, *"Disgraziato!"*

"Better keep your girls inside," I cautioned Mrs. Palmieri when she opened the door to their camper in hair curlers, wearing a kimono robe over a leotard and tights. I kept looking for any sign of Alessandro and ran off down the midway, following the trail of Fritz and his dogs.

Just as the water truck came into view, I heard the heavy sound of fists landing on a body. The air became electric as a man's screams grew louder. The noise and commotion was quick, like a series of explosions, and then everything fell silent. Crawling on top of a truck cab to get a panoramic view of the scene, I watched as the water boy ran for his life in his underwear across an open field.

At a whistle, Fritz's Eskimo dogs charged after Wayne; they ran at a fast clip in formation, brandishing their bushy white tails in the air like weapons. They snapped and barked, and the lead dog nipped at Wayne's pale legs as they herded their quarry to the highway. Then they circled and returned to their owner, showing all of their wolfish teeth, tongues hanging out to one side.

I saw Jesse sidle up to West in the midway and call out some kind of inside joke for all to hear: "I never did understand what you saw in that crazy-ass water boy, or maybe it was the other way around, huh?"

West looked daggers at Jesse and then turned and headed back to the elephant truck. Then, all at once, it was quiet again. Mr. Palmieri appeared in the distance, walking smoothly toward the midway, gripping his son's upper arm. The boy was in his underwear. The clown followed them calmly, his six dogs trotting obediently beside him, three on each side.

Mrs. Palmieri ran toward her husband and lifted her fearful blue eyes to meet his. *"Ma, cos'è successo?"*

"I'll tell you what happened! *Gli spacco la faccia, quel maledetto di Dio,"* the acrobat father snarled. His clenched fist trembled in the air.

A group of performers came out of their campers and began to gather. The news traveled across the lot in minutes. Deuce caught Wayne, the water boy, trying to fondle the eleven-year-old acrobat boy in the cab of his truck. The muscle-bound tattooed roustabout was seen jumping through the cab window feet first, kicking the water boy in the face with his boot heels as he yelled at Alessandro to get the hell out of there. Then Mr. Palmieri arrived on the scene, and the two men dragged the screaming water boy out of the truck along with the *Batman Thirtieth Anniversary* comic book he had used to lure the young boy. Deuce landed a couple of punches as soon as Wayne fell to the ground, but the water boy managed to scramble away and took off. Soon enough, the Spitz dogs arrived, and the chase was on.

The keys to the water truck were left hanging in the ignition. No one ever repeated the stern warning that we all heard the father deliver in shouts to his son inside their camper. There was no gossip, no scandal. Circus performers and the hardscrabble collection of misfits who did the hard labor lived in close quarters day after day, in all kinds of weather. Justice was meted out within the circus on its own terms. Wayne had crossed the line, and he was gone—an outcast among outcasts—thrown to the dogs. He became a non-person, and no one on performers' row ever saw him or heard his name mentioned again.

As for the beautiful blond-haired acrobat boy, Alessandro continued to show up for school without fail, as if nothing had happened. He waited for his youngest sister to pack up her things each time a session ended, and they all disappeared together behind the tent flap out onto the midway. On the surface, everything seemed to have returned to normal, but I noticed that the old German circus clown set up his dog run next to the Palmieri's camper for the rest of the season to keep watch over the children.

★ ★ ★

That night, I pretended to sleep when West slipped out around midnight. After a few minutes, I opened our sleeper door, slid down onto the truck engine, and jumped down to the ground. I could see West heading for the open road at the far end of the lot. He held a bundle in one hand. I melted into the woods and watched as he approached a public phone booth, still lit up, next to a gas station. A man emerged from the shadows from the back of the building. It was Wayne. Had he been hiding in the rest room the whole time? West gave him the parcel, and the water boy's head bobbed. West made an angry gesture with one arm and walked away quickly in sweeping strides.

The truth was scratching at the back of my mind like a rat in the wall. Jesse had said something about the water boy to West that made me wonder if they had a pact of some kind, something beyond the drug smuggling, something lewd and sexual. Or was West merely showing mercy by handing the water boy a set of fresh clothes? Before I could get a good look, West was halfway across the field. I had to hightail it back to the sleeper to reach it before he did. I began to pray that West hadn't seen me running in the night.

DEEP SOUTH

9

"Do you really love him, or do you just love the life he leads?" Lily, Billy Gunga's wife from the Philippines, stretched out her long, tan legs and leaned back on a folding lounge chair outside her camper. She took a deep drag on a cigarette and turned her head toward me; I sat in the lounge chair next to hers. I had confided in her my doubts about West. I was blowing hot and cold on our relationship. Now that I knew a little more about him—the drug dealing, his involvement with Wayne and Jesse and their "sketchy business," as he called it—I wasn't so sure he was the magical nature boy who had entranced me in the beginning.

"I think maybe I've fallen in love with the circus more than anything else. I'm grateful, indebted to West because he's the one who helped me join the show. And I like the place I get to be—here with you all, traveling with the show—because West likes me," I said, surprised at my own confession.

Lily tilted her chin up, blew a stream of smoke into the air, and tapped her Virginia Extra Slim on the armrest, flicking off the ash. "Sometimes it's hard to distinguish between the two loves: the circus man or the circus life."

Her words haunted me all morning as I prepared my toys for sale. I loved my life with the circus; it was unfolding in real time. I was really living now, not waiting for something exciting to happen to me. A new morning brought a new place to explore, different people to meet and playact for. I was part of the circus mystique.

I spotted a couple of townies looking at me through their binoculars while I swept out our sleeper in my fanciful Rajasthani getup, my hair covered in a colorful orange-and-red scarf trimmed with dime-sized mirrors. The two men were old-timers, sitting up on a bluff overlooking the lot, bags of popcorn in their laps. Their curiosity pleased me, so I decided to put on a show for them and began exaggerating my movements.

West sauntered by shirtless on his way back from rinsing off at the water truck. An open gaping tear in his work pants revealed a smooth section of butt cheek. The men trained their binoculars on the two of us, and I gesticulated and called out to West in a made-up language for the benefit of the onlookers. I wanted them to imagine us as Hungarian Romany lovers reunited after a quarrel. West took on his part seamlessly; he flung his hand in the air and shouted gibberish back to me; then he faced me sturdily with his feet planted apart, hands on his hips.

We played these little theatrical games with variations for townies both on and off the lot. West and I were often exotically dressed in old costumes I had borrowed or mended. Once, we got into such a heated argument in our invented language that when I raised a broom to hit West over the head, he reacted by grabbing a whip out of the elephant trailer, took aim, and gave it a good crack right at my feet. He missed me, but the tip of the whip leather landed so close to the edge of my long skirt that I felt a gust of hot air and dirt at my ankles. The surprise and shock of it made me laugh uncontrollably, and I broke character, nearly wetting my pants.

"You're pretty good with that thing," I said, once I'd recovered.

"Got to be."

"Why? You never use a whip in the ring." I wondered if the ringmaster had been training him.

"Not on the elephants, Sarah." West seemed determined to tease me. "Come on, what other animals are we taking to South America?"

"Big cats? Really?" I looked at him in amazement.

"I got over a thousand dollars saved up now, so I can start over with a clean slate. I'm thinking Colombia or maybe Argentina."

"You're serious?"

"Aren't you?" The circus boy's eyes met mine, but they weren't smiling. I detected a fleeting look of sadness.

* * *

That night, I copied out a passage from the book of Ruth in the Bible, which some old circus bum had left behind in the antique dresser in our sleeper: "Intreat me not to leave thee, *or* to return from following after thee: for whither thou goest, I will go; and where thou lodgest, I will lodge; thy people shall be my people, and thy God, my God."

I pinned the folded-up paper with these words on the underside of the top bunk, so West would be sure to see the note when he turned in. The kerosene lamp glowed in the corner, its light reflecting in the mirror over the dresser. I quickly fished for my sewing kit in the top drawer of the bureau and selected my sharpest little scissors. I leaned to one side, held the end of my long braid in front of me, and clipped off the crescent-shaped tip. With a single thread, I bound the lock of hair together and folded it inside the note. I wanted West to believe in me. I think maybe I also wanted to convince myself that I would follow him to South America—that such a turn in my life was possible.

After counting up the change and stacking the bills by denomination in neat little piles on the bed, I calculated my twenty percent commission for my total take for the week and then made out the list of sold inventory to give to Margarita after breakfast the next day. I always sold enough to keep a twenty, thanks to the crisp one-hundred-dollar bill from the man I began to call *Sugar Granddaddy* in my head. The sale of the giant teddy bear at the end of the show had become my bread and butter.

I joined West around eleven at night, toward the end of teardown, when the canvas had been wound up on the large mechanical spool, ready to be unfurled and opened up in sections at the next lot. The lights were loaded last, but there was always one spotlight left on in the middle of the field. The open meadow was so inviting on that balmy night. The elephants became excited and made rumbling noises to each other, communicating in their own intimate way. West bent over and took their foot chains off. Bessie bobbed her head and nuzzled the circus boy's chest with her trunk.

"It's okay, Bessie," he spoke to her gently. "You and Mary deserve a break. Go on."

The female pachyderms wandered off together, playing tag by intermittently touching each other's trunks before linking them up. They strolled down the field, the domes of their noble heads close together like two old friends lost in conversation.

"You let them loose like that?" I looked at West in disbelief.

"Hey, no one is going to see them. All the townies have gone home."

"Yeah, but what if they run away?" I watched the humps of their backs get smaller and smaller as they ambled off in the smoky mist.

"They're not going anywhere. Elephants are just like us—they like to hang out with their friends and relax after work." At a distance, I watched the female elephants exploring the dense foliage and snapping tree branches, always side by side. They flapped their ears slowly, contented with their lush surroundings.

I helped West load the last of the equipment onto the light truck, grateful for the clear moonlit night that let me see in the dark. The two elephants had become a large gray shape at the far end of the field.

"Watch this," said West. He put two fingers in his mouth and whistled in a loud shrieking burst. The elephants' ears came forward to a horizontal position at once.

"Come, Mary. Come, Bessie," the elephant trainer commanded in a voice brought up from the lowest register of the diaphragm. The two elephants broke into a full run and joyfully stampeded across the meadow at top speed, which was eighteen miles an hour, according to Red.

"Here they come!" West clapped his hands and whistled again.

"Jesus, West, they're going to trample us!" I shrank back behind the light truck, fearful that Bessie and Mary wouldn't slow down as they approached us. The ground shook underfoot, as if a herd of cattle was coming through.

"Hold up, Bessie. Hold up, Mary." West raised one palm in the air, and the elephants slowed their gait, resuming their meandering pace. They sidled up to their trainer, creaking and rumbling, as if they were telling West all about their exciting adventure.

I understood why they loved him so much. West had always been able to read their thoughts and found ways to reward them for every favor he asked of them. He had earned their trust this way, by being fair. Bessie and Mary were his.

★ ★ ★

It seemed as though the farther south we traveled the more things fell apart. We had played all the small towns in Virginia from Marion to Galax, and we were headed into some steep country on our way to North Carolina. West parked the truck on a treacherous incline so that we could get out and take a long look at the Blue Ridge Mountains swimming into view through the morning fog, but it was a mistake. The tires began to give way and slide back on a road slick with the previous night's rain. West hopped up into the driver's seat and pulled hard on the emergency brake. I ran to the back of the truck, removed the chock block from the rear wheel, ran with it tucked under my arm up to the front of the truck, and jumped in the cab just as West hit the accelerator. I almost didn't make it in. We were moving rapidly uphill as I closed the passenger door.

"I had my chance," West teased, once we found ourselves on a flat open road again, "if I'd wanted to red-light you."

"You would have ditched me?"

"Never. Not here, not at a traffic light. Not ever." He grabbed me behind the neck, pulled me across the seat, and kissed me.

During the evening show in North Wilkesboro that night, I didn't sell any toys in the ring, not one. I couldn't believe it. I had tried everything: scanning the crowd for a flicker of movement, targeting sections of children with enthusiastic expressions, and using my best loud circus voice. Round and round I went, all along the edge of the rings, calling up into the bleachers, "Get your circus toys here! Circus toys! Only one dollar!" These circus-goers were the most hard-hearted people I'd ever encountered on the road. Sales began to dwindle, and I wondered if I needed to change my routine. In the North, people seated in the stands wanted me to keep my distance. I had always seen hawkers work crowds this way, within signaling distance, but never up close, face to face.

Three days and three jumps later, during our last performance in North Carolina in Waynesville, I changed my sales tactics: I went right up to people in the bleachers, section by section, and personally asked them in a sweet Southern accent, "Would you like to buy a circus toy? Only seventy-five cents for the small ones here." This personal approach seemed to be expected. Margarita added Confederate flags to my stock, and I ended up selling more toys in the Deep South than anywhere in the North.

Here the circus was special, magical. A mother asked me to kiss her daughter who was going into the hospital for heart surgery the next day. Still, the South was the South, and I didn't belong in Dixie. The few black roustabouts that had joined us in New

England had disappeared from the show. I was learning words I'd never heard before, like "high yella" and "jiggaboo." My northern accent was buried, along with my Yankee roots, as I tried to present myself as an exotic foreigner. Outside our sleeper truck, I would sit on the truck engine and sew, a transistor radio that looked like a Budweiser beer can propped up on the truck hood. The only radio stations we could get played gospel music and I hummed along with the lyrics: "Put your hand in the hand of the man from Galilee."

Whenever West and I walked to town or went into a store, eyes followed us, and we continued our charade of being circus people from distant lands. We put on accents, spoke in gibberish, and emphasized our speech with dramatic hand gestures.

After a particularly good night with my toy sales, we made a trip into town right after setup the next day with money to burn. I cruised among the bolts of cloth in the sewing section, looking through packets of paper patterns for an *Arabian Nights*-themed Halloween costume. I wanted to make myself a pair of harem pants to match my vest of Rajasthani mirrors. I picked up some gold brocade and fingered lustrous gauze I could envision floating off my hips below the navel. The poppy-colored red silk would fan out in multiple folds of soft pleats around my legs and gather at the ankle. I imagined my midriff and the curve of my belly on display. All I needed was one of Lily's sequined brassieres to wear under my red-and-yellow striped Rajasthani vest.

West caught up with me, holding some beef jerky and a long bowie knife. He laughed to see me unfold the long remnant of discounted red silk to measure it by eye.

"Look at us," he said. "We're such complete opposites. You are a beautiful maiden from the Renaissance, and me?" He held up his intended purchases, the bowie knife in one hand and the beef jerky in the other. West let out a hearty laugh. "I'm a cave man!"

We were different … in every way, I thought. A love story of opposites: North meets South; rich meets poor. It thrilled me to think that West and I could transcend such powerful forces as class and culture.

What made all our social differences disappear was our common ability to inhabit other personalities. I could put on a costume, an accent, and a new set of behaviors and become a woman of my own creation. West would do the same, enjoying the different roles we played as a couple. It was possible to reinvent ourselves and shed the skins of our previous lives. In the South, we were more alike than different because of our common bond as circus people: our life on the road, our friendships with theatrical foreigners, and our devotion to the wild animals in our care. We defied conservative Southern conventions by wearing our hair loose and long. I never wore a bra, and West always went commando under his jumpsuit, making for quick and easy costume changes, among other things. And to be honest, maybe the occasional hit of marijuana in the truck helped diminish our social differences too. There were no barriers between us when we were high. We were just man and woman then: Adam and Eve.

★ ★ ★

One afternoon, I tried to rest before the four o'clock show, but it was so hot in the lower bunk I had to edge my shoulder away from the metal wall in the sleeper truck to avoid getting burned. It was as hot as a flat iron. I already had a little half-moon scar where I'd seared my skin. Hot and irritable, I threw my sleeping bag on the ground outside and jumped out onto the grass to join West, wearing nothing under my overalls but a skimpy tube top. He was resting on a blanket under the truck where it was nice and cool; now and then a fresh breeze would blow through bringing in a scent of cut grass and diesel. I made a spot for myself on top of my sleeping bag and settled down next to him. He reached over and began to draw his index finger over the tender flesh up my side and under my bare arm. I held still, wondering if his gentle caress would evolve into a tickle fight. Soon I was giggling and twisting away from him.

When Lefèvre found me there, he dragged me out from under the truck like a rabbit by tugging hard at the corners of my sleeping bag. "People," he explained in his French accent, "get the wrong idea."

This was one of the first times the ringmaster had spoken to me directly. His disapproval confused me. This was not the first time I'd wriggled under one of the trucks to nap beside West. Now I was made to feel like a wayward daughter brought to heel.

Later West told me that two policemen had seen me scramble under the truck in my overalls and had questioned Lefèvre about what I was doing there. "This is Alabama. Here, we get lots of heat from the law." West put his arm around my shoulder and spoke softly into my ear, "And maybe you should ditch the overalls and put on a dress or something."

"Why?"

"It's the South. They don't like boys who look like girls or girls who look like boys, you know?"

I had heard plenty about Governor George Wallace and the bitter prejudices of the conservative South. In fact, I had been a bit surprised to find there were as many longhairs in the South as there were in the North. Southern rockers, like the Allman Brothers and Johnny Winter, had made it cool for everyone, not just the "leftie communist hippies up North" to let their freedom flag fly.

For young men, letting their hair grow to their shoulders was a real act of defiance. The traditional crew cut still showed support for US armed forces in Vietnam, even if it included the bombing of Cambodia, the use of Agent Orange and whatever else "Tricky Dick" Nixon put over on the nation. Down here, anyone who didn't support the war in Vietnam was considered a flag-burning traitor.

Back in Massachusetts, lots of cars had bumper stickers: "Make love, not war." But the American flag decal on a windshield signaled the opposite political point of view: "Nuke 'em!" It made it complicated to show one's patriotism by displaying an American flag. On Memorial Day, my siblings and I had protested and asked my parents not to hang the flag out on the porch, not until the US was out of Vietnam. My brothers had managed to avoid the draft—two on college deferment—and the oldest, as a conscientious objector. "Hell no, we won't go," was the chant at every demonstration. I was already wary of the police. At fifteen, I had learned to protect myself from teargas at anti-war rallies by soaking a scarf in water and holding it over my face.

As hot as those summer days were, the political climate in the early seventies was even hotter. In the Deep South, it was getting harder and harder for Reyes Bros. to negotiate a space where circus people could be treated with respect. I imagined that we were regarded as potential thieves and prostitutes, with a cooch tent or a peep show for libidinous men—just like the train circuses of the past. It didn't help that many in our entourage came from other countries and spoke with an accent. It seemed to me the cops were always coming around to watch us set up now. I wondered if they were looking for someone in particular. They waddled about the lot, thumbs in their belt loops, proud of their sunglasses and the broad-brimmed hats that shaded their faces.

Our ability to blend in with the local scene in Alabama was about to be tested. A real day off was coming up. I was looking forward to it. Then maybe I could take a real shower with *all* my clothes off. With the police poking about the back yard and scrutinizing any unladylike behavior, it was difficult for me to bathe in the open by the water truck.

West and I began to make plans to stay at a motel with a swimming pool in town. Some of the other performers were doing the same. I could already imagine savoring the long, hot bath followed by a cool dip in the pool.

★ ★ ★

We went to room eleven, which we called Deuce's room be-cause he had made the reservation, but we had agreed to share the time. West and I would take the afternoon, and Deuce could have the evening for a tryst with a townie woman. On our way down the hall with the room key, we ran headlong into the manager hustling two roustabouts with long hair out of a room.

"I don't rent my rooms to girls," he sneered and held out his hand. "That'll be two dollars each for messing up the beds."

West and I ducked into our room, which we had for four hours, and we made use of every minute. We tore off our clothes and jumped in the shower. Then, with washed, wet hair dripping down our backs, we made love. West wrapped a gauzy white shower curtain around my soapy body like a Grecian robe and entered from behind. This time I felt my body pulse and release in a natural climax.

"I liked that," I smiled over my shoulder at West when we stepped out of the shower.

"Yeah, me too. I liked the … uh …"

"Choreography!" I interjected, and we howled with laughter.

"Hey, let's lie out on the bed—naked, under the fan," West suggested. "But put your towel underneath you. We got to leave the bed in good shape for Deuce and his lady friend."

We were so spent we fell asleep while the ceiling fan wafted overhead, drying our bodies. I woke up after about an hour, feel-ing cold and clammy, and I went back into the bathroom to draw a hot bath. West had wrapped a towel around his waist. He sat at the little pine writing desk in the corner with an ounce baggy of grass and a packet of EZ Wider rolling papers.

"Bring the joint in here," I called, leaning out the bathroom door, with my hair falling at an angle in long, damp strings. "A bubble bath is going to feel amazing. Like when we were kids." Then we sat face to face in the warm water, passing a joint back and forth between us. As soon as we got down to the roach, we made love again in the tub. All was blissful pleasure and playful splashing. West made up love poems that sent me into paroxysms of giggles.

With your lovely eyes
And hair like flaxen
Don't you know
You make me feel like relaxin'?

Once outside by the pool, I suddenly felt shy about my body. I had no bathing suit, but I had borrowed a leotard. The juggling twins, Alana and Carla, rested easily on lounge chairs; they were not quite identical. Alana was the tall one with a well-developed muscular frame and the mature face of a grown woman, while Carla seemed almost pixie-like with her slight build, dimples, and pretty turned-up nose. Both were slim and elastic. Alana could do a back bend from a standing position, grab her ankles, and pull her head through her feet. I liked the way they wore their long blonde pony tails, drawn up through little cone hats. Their hair extensions flew through the air behind them when they did their aerial act on the ladder.

I felt awkward and exposed as I stood there blinking in the bright sunlight. "I always feel self-conscious when I wear a leotard," I confided.

"Really?" said Alana simply. "I never feel that way."

"You don't?" I insisted. Their costumes were so revealing, and the twins and I were almost the same age. If I'd had to wear their costumes, I would have been even more self-conscious. My body was what I would call good but not great. I had a strong, sleek upper body and long tapered legs, but lately I'd noticed my thickening middle and little round belly that wouldn't go away. I'd had too many free Cokes and "government issue" at Blacky's cookhouse. When I couldn't stand another canned yam, he would let me take the white bread and the gallon drum of peanut butter off his stock shelf and make myself a sandwich.

"We've been doing this for so long, we just don't think about it," concluded Carla, the practical twin. She got up from the lounge chair, stretched her arms over her head with locked fingers, and then dropped her arms by her side and stepped into the pool. Her sister headed for the high diving board. I had seen the two of them practicing side by side in the center ring between the shows while I was tutoring the children.

"I'd like to try the ladder some time. I love to swing up high in the air," I ventured. "I do it all the time at home. We have a big maple tree." I had even mastered jumping out of the swing in mid-air. I had miscalculated only once when I was eleven, scraping my shins so badly that I rushed to my room to hide the two long tracks of blood under a pair of woolen knee socks. I was found out in short order when my mother took me to buy shoes. "When are you going to learn to act like a little lady?" she'd sighed.

When I'm dead, I thought.

Alana bubbled up to the surface after executing a perfect swan dive into the deep end of the pool. "Come on over after you finish teaching the kids," she called over to me as I stepped up on the diving board. "We can get you up on the ladder."

Carla bobbed over to her sister in the center of the pool. The twins smiled up at me and then turned their pony-tailed blond heads in profile and beamed at each other. In perfect synchronicity, each circus girl took a gulp of air and ducked under the water where they performed identical, side-by-side handstands. I watched their pointed toes emerge first, and then their long ballerina legs rose up out of the water. Their dainty feet appeared to glide away from me as they walked on their hands underwater back to the shallow end.

Then it was my turn at the high dive. I went in head first, springing up off my toes and into the air. The cold water crashed against my skull as I entered the water and shot in a swirl of limbs to the bottom of the pool. When I pawed my way up to the surface, I took a big gulp of air. My head was tingling. Crashing the water's surface had ruined my high, but I wasn't sorry. My mind was perfectly clear. I felt exhilarated, as if I had broken through to a hidden truth.

FLYING THROUGH THE AIR

10

I took the twins up on their offer the very next day. "Hep!" and I was jump-lifted up into the ladder, and I seated myself on the bottom rung. Swede, our spotter, pulled on the rope fastened to the ladder, and I began to swing higher and higher. Soon I was flying—leg muscles popping, toes pointing, white-knuckled fingers holding on tight to the rung at chest height.

The ladder swooped in a generous arc. At full momentum, my toes touched the roof of the big top tent before plummeting back toward the center of the ring. There was no net. Some performers who were learning new aerial tricks used a mechanic as a safety device, but our circus didn't have one. It didn't matter to me; I wasn't afraid at all. I liked nothing better than flying on the highest reaching swing I had ever tried in my life. The air rushed over my body as I let go with one hand, stretched out my arm, and leaned back in a full layout on my return descent.

After that first lesson, I showed up every afternoon, chalking my hands before grabbing the bar. I convinced Margarita to join me, and we became students of the lead trapeze artist, Mirabella. Mirabella was married to Swede, and as long he was in the ring looking up, checking the rigging as our bodies flashed through the air, we felt safe. And he was always there to catch us in his massive arms. Every day Swede checked for high humidity as we traveled deeper into the South. Accumulated moisture on the bar could cause deadly accidents.

Mirabella's most dangerous trick came at the very end of her act when she hung upside down from the trapeze by her heels. The ringmaster would underscore this feat by declaring into the microphone, "The aerial artistry of *Mira-bell-ah!*" Usually, the applause would drown him out before he could finish.

I liked to have something to hold on to at all times, and I learned to use a loop around my wrist and later, my foot, to do various "hang out" tricks. After a few weeks, Margarita and I could do a simple routine with a full-body layout on the return swing. Once we had mastered basic tricks that we could perform while seated, we progressed to aerial ballet tricks that involved dangling our bodies in graceful poses in midair. These were risky to attempt barehanded, especially on humid days when the sweat could make us lose our grip. Mirabella insisted that we use the loop, a kind of thick, soft rope in the form of a noose, which could be tightened around one wrist with a little leather sleeve.

Once my wrist was secure inside the loop, I would reach up with the same hand and wrap my fingers around the neck of the noose until my knuckles blanched. Then my attachment to the top rung of the ladder—at least by one hand—was assured. My free hand was placed several rungs down, and when I extricated my legs from the ladder, I would push the apparatus away from my body with both hands. My arms would form a "V" over my head, as if I were performing a sideways bench press. With arms raised and the ladder away from my body, my legs were free to make splits, arabesques, and stag poses, while Swede kept the ladder swinging by pulling on the ropes below.

"Now," coached Mirabella, "you have to do all those tricks with your left hand in the loop."

"Shit," I said, looking over at Margarita on the other ladder (she was also breathing hard). "I'm still learning to hoist myself up into the ladder without Swede's help."

The twins made it look so easy. From a confident standing position beneath side-by-side metal ladders dangling overhead, they sprang up and snatched the bottom rung with both hands in unison. Then they would tuck their knees to their chests, pull their legs through, and drape them over the bar. With one quick contraction, Alana and Carla both were seated upright, their toes pointed and their faces flashing bright circus smiles. They completed the mount in seconds.

"Backflips, Sarah. Once you do a hundred, they're much easier." And then Mirabella had me hang by the knees from the bottom rung and do a set of sit-ups for good measure before dismounting.

The more I practiced the aerial routines, the more I felt free of my dependence on West. I had been clinging to him as my lifeline to the circus, intent on winning his approval by playing the dutiful housewife, mending his costumes, and sweeping out our sleeper while he was working under the big top. Now that I was finding my feet at the circus and on my way to becoming a performer, things started to come apart with West. The less I depended on him to justify my presence on the lot, the more he turned on me. Once, I failed to wake him up in time for his entrance because Margarita and I were practicing backflips over at the Palmieri camper. I made my excuse, but we argued anyway.

"I'm not around here just because you don't have an alarm clock," I said, maybe a bit too playfully.

"Don't bitch at *me*," the elephant trainer growled. "Why don't you go join women's lib, so you can snap your fingers at people!" I could feel him trying to cut me down with his voice. The lack of sleep made both of us vulnerable to streaks of bad temper, I had to admit.

Something strange was happening to us. One night, we both had nightmares and woke each other up by talking to each other in our sleep. West was making clumsy mistakes now, missing a step and falling to the ground if he left the sleeper in a hurry, and sometimes he forgot the clubs and other props he liked to use in the ring. Often he would blame me. "You got some kind of witchcraft thing going on; you're giving me the evil eye or something."

★ ★ ★

West was going off on his own into the hills for hours at a time. He said he just wanted to get back to himself. Leave the "goddamn corrupt circus" for a little while. I came to understand that the natural world was where West really lived, and these forays into the local wilderness made me respect him more. Still, I sensed he was on edge, even when he returned from spending time in the hills.

Maybe he was just short of sleep, I thought. He was now doing the job of two men: performing in the ring and working the elephants during setup and teardown. Some mornings when we arrived on the lot, they were calling for an elephant before he had downed a cup of coffee from the cookhouse.

The ringmaster had stepped up our circus schedule too. Some days, we ended up wildcatting our way into new territory, booking shows on short notice in towns that hadn't been visited by other circuses or carneys, just to make a little extra. The old route had too many long jumps, and we had run out of drivers, so we zigzagged from state to state, crossing from Alabama into Tennessee, to play in Athens, Crossville, McMinnville, and Tullahoma before heading south again to Bridgeport, Alabama.

So many roustabouts were leaving the show that it was impossible to get all the trucks to the lot on time without sending some roustabouts back by car to make the jump a second time in one day. Drivers were sleep-deprived. Equipment broke down. Tempers flared. Even the spool truck caught fire.

It was during those hard-bitten days and sleepless nights that I found myself fighting with West almost daily. A current of fear and tension was simmering just below the surface among the crew. Under the big top during setup, I overheard the roustabouts muttering angry words under their breath, but I couldn't lay a finger on what was wrong. Late at night, West would prowl the lot, always taking a knife with him.

One night, I woke up to the grating sound of a closing zipper, pulled in a hurry. West was up and in his circus coveralls.

"Why are you doing that?" I mumbled sleepily.

"Doing what?" West slipped a blade into the deep side pocket on his pant leg.

"Going off at night with a fucking knife. What the hell is going on?"

"You really want to know? I don't think so."

"What the hell? Of course I want to know."

"There's shit going down, that's all I can say. Whatever you see me do, you just keep it to yourself. I mean it."

To make matters worse, I had now missed a period and began to look with concern at the lack of red Xs marking off my menstrual cycle on the Ganesh calendar on the wall of our sleeper. I hadn't marked off any days in September. We were never in one place for more than a day except on Sundays when we'd stay put for our day off, and that was every two weeks now. When the first store-bought pregnancy test was negative, I was relieved, chalking up my irregularity to life on the road. I was never settled, a bird away from its nest for too long. But a worry slipped into my head. Should I have used more protection than a diaphragm when we were having sex in the tub back at that motel? The intimacy and luxury had all felt so good after so many days of hard living. I assured myself that I had checked my calendar. I was still on day ten in my cycle back then, too early to worry about getting pregnant.

I tried calling home once during a layover, but our Scottish housekeeper, Mabel, answered the phone. Had I forgotten that my parents were in New Haven visiting my brothers for the Harvard-Yale football game? I'd responded testily that no, I wouldn't need the telephone number to reach them at the Yale Club later that evening. Instead, I left the message that I was just fine. "Okay, sweetie pie," Mabel had said gaily. I was still a child in her eyes.

★ ★ ★

Two weeks later, we had another layover in Warner Robins, Georgia. It had been a beautiful day, with children crowding around to see "them big old elephants." After the crowds dispersed, West and I clambered up on Bessie's hairy back and rode her down to the river. The other elephant, Mary, followed patiently behind. We lurched along slowly, listening to the female elephant's contented squeaking as she spied the shimmering water, the far bank shaded by lush trees and overhanging Spanish moss. In we went, the water reaching our knees before we slithered off the elephant's back. Bessie showered us with a trunkful of water in what became a game of splash tag. West splashed her back, shoveling water from the surface with both arms. All at once, Mary broke away in a fit of jealousy and ran up the grassy embankment.

"Mary!" West called after her, but Bessie sprayed him with another trunkful of water, and several minutes passed before we were able to ride her out of the river, seated one behind the other on her thick neck. West held me around the waist with such tenderness that I wondered if he guessed I'd had my blood drawn for a pregnancy test at the emergency room that morning.

"Now where the hell is that crazy old elephant?" he said, scanning the horizon. There were a few houses off a dirt road at the edge of the fields.

"Uh oh," said West, just as I heard a woman's screams electrify the air.

"It's coming from over there!" I pointed to a white farm house with a wraparound front porch. Bessie had already broken into a trot, and she trumpeted noisily as we bumped along in the direction of the commotion.

A farmer's wife, wearing an apron over a checkered dress and a rag to cover her disheveled hair, came running out of her house with a broom and lit into us.

"Get your big old elephant out my kitchen!"

"I apologize for the inconvenience, ma'am," said West, sliding off Bessie's back and approaching Mary with an outstretched hand. Her trunk was roving through the open kitchen window, smelling whatever was left out on the counter.

"Inconvenience, you call it? I almost died of fright when that big old thing come to my window box and snatched up all my nasturtiums."

"I'm sorry about the flowers, ma'am." West was already up on Mary's broad back. "I'll have the ringmaster send you all some free tickets to the show."

The farmer's wife gave us a crooked smile, changing her indignant tone to one of shared amusement. "Well, I already seen a pretty good show right here at my own house! That elephant of yours raised up the kitchen window and put her trunk straight into my sink full of soaking dishes!"

"Did she spray anybody?" West asked, as he leaned over and calmed Mary by stroking her behind the ears.

"No, but I wish she'd spray my husband when he come in from the barn!"

We all had a good laugh over that one.

★ ★ ★

I took a long walk into town in the afternoon to pick up the results of my blood test at the hospital. It surprised me that a doctor would congratulate a seventeen-year-old girl so enthusiastically. "You're going to be a mother!" But maybe he didn't know my age. And maybe, by then, I looked a lot older. Or maybe girls just got started a lot earlier in Georgia. Blushing with surprise, I managed to utter an appropriately shy thank you.

All the way back, I apologized to God for what I knew I would have to do. I did not question if I should—only how I would. I had tried not to get pregnant. I had counted days, used protection, and he had cooperated by staying away at peak times of risk. But the blind forces of nature that had drawn us together had won out. Our love child was a fact of life, as inevitable as a wave hitting the shore.

That afternoon, I stopped at a phone booth and made long distance calls with a handful of loose quarters from my toy sales. I got through to an eight-hundred number for Planned Parenthood. Next came the call home, brief and to the point. Yes, I was fine. No, I wouldn't be taking any college courses in September. Yes, I would be coming home at the end of the tour. I couldn't say more. Letting my parents in on my secret was out of the question. And I never revealed how much I missed home, so much that I had taken to buying little jars of baby food at convenience stores—Blueberry Buckle and Raspberry Cobbler— just to taste a little comfort.

SWAMP RAT

11

eardown took too long. It was almost two o'clock in the morning when West returned to the sleeper. I thought he'd be dead tired, but his body was rippling with nervous energy. While I waited in bed, he leaned against the bureau, pulling off his boots in impatient, jerky motions.

"So?" he said. "You going to tell me if you're pregnant, or do I just get to stand here like a scarecrow?"

"I am."

"You're pregnant." He lowered his chin and looked at me for confirmation.

"Yeah, but I'm not keeping it."

"Just like that." He bolted upright, his back as straight as razor wire. "You don't feel anything? What the hell is the matter with you?"

I got up slowly and faced him. "What did you think I would do?" I said softly, fingering the tassels that tied on his costume cape. He handed the black cloak to me, and I hung it on the clothesline we had strung up in the corner. As West slid the sequin-studded satin shirt off his bare torso, I felt a twinge, the old attraction coming back. "It's not like we're going to get married," I offered.

"That's a load of crap. You don't want to keep it because you can't love me." I knew I could no longer hide behind my words. He was coming at me, claws out.

"That's not the reason," I protested. "I'm a child myself. I can't be having a baby now. I wouldn't know what to do with it."

"Like, you'd be the first girl in the universe to have a child. Come on. Why don't you tell me the truth for once?" West's sarcastic tone had taken root, and his eyes darkened.

"That *is* the truth. How am I going to go to college with a baby? Are you kidding?"

"Oh, that's news! You're going to college? Nice of you to let me in on your little secret. So what *was* all this?" The circus boy made a sweeping gesture around the walls of our sleeper, his arm outstretched. "Just a game so you could join the circus?"

"Well, I'm pregnant. It's not a game now," I said.

"But all along, you knew you'd be leaving, right?" West narrowed his eyes and peered into my face. His vicious expression began to frighten me.

"I never said anything about staying on with you after we reached winter quarters," I said in my defense. I reached out to touch his shoulder. "I'm here now. And I want to ride it out, all the way to the end."

He angled out of my reach, and, all at once, he raged at me. "So I'm just your ticket to the show. You *bitch*. All your lovemaking is just an act. You didn't even lose your virginity for the right reason, you *whore*."

I slapped West right across the face. It happened on impulse, just like that. But the circus boy was quick, and he grabbed my hand, pulled it up hard behind my back, and pushed me over double. The flat of his hand came down hard on my backside again and again. He was spanking me, but our physical struggle was so frightening, I cried out in real terror in peals of fear and rage. How far would he go?

"You've got to start acting more like a lady," he said tersely.

"Stop your crying. It's just a spanking. It's what you deserve—it's nothing. I've *killed* a man for less than you've done."

Those words sent a bolt of fear through my body. He slapped me hard until I fell limp, hoping that would make him stop. Seeing my body lying there looking lifeless in our bed seemed to sicken him, and he moved off me and stood up. "Stop doing that," his voice was hoarse. "It makes me want to puke."

West had never hit me before. Doors were opening on possibilities I never knew existed. I remained curled up for several minutes, until I realized that he was not going to use his fists. "Go ahead," I mumbled through tears. "Kill me." It was an empty challenge. I could tell by his voice that the storm had passed. But I knew he was capable of doing me much more harm. He had decided not to.

"Don't think I couldn't." West spoke serenely even as vicious truths poured out of his mouth. "I've shoved girls up against concrete walls. I *know* I'm no good."

I felt the depth of the dark place we had fallen into, and I looked at West—a stranger to me now. "What has *happened* to you? How could you raise a hand to me? You don't even treat your elephants that way." My voice was thick with tears.

"You don't know shit!" West growled between his teeth, but he had lowered his hand, and his shoulders slumped. All the tension seemed to melt out of his body as he hunched forward and slowly unzipped his dress pants, stepped out of the pool of clothing at his feet, and kicked the pile into a corner. He sat down on the bed next to me and rested his head in his hands.

West was crying softly now. I listened to him with my eyes closed. His voice broke when he said, "I just thought that maybe, *maybe* this time, something good had come into my life. That was you, Sarah. You sewing a button on my shirt, you walking by my side into town, and you waiting for me back at the sleeper after teardown, opening up your arms to let me under the covers, even when you were half asleep. Don't you see what that means to someone like me—the one no one expects to amount to anything?

"You have no idea who I am. If you did, you wouldn't even be here." The circus boy was completely naked. He lay down beside me, exhausted, as if he had been pummeled in a brawl. I put my palm on his hairless chest and rested my head on his shoulder.

"I don't care. I want to know who you really are," I said, through tears, forcing myself to calm down. "If you love me, you won't be afraid to tell me." I was pressing for more assurances, for no reason in particular other than a nagging fear in the center of my abdomen. I didn't want to feel it, but it was there, telling me to run for my life. *I'm overreacting*, I thought. *I'm imagining things.*

The circus boy stretched out next to me and wrapped his arm around my shoulder. I could see the high cheekbones, the smooth planes of his face in the orange half-light of the kerosene lamp.

"I'm just a bastard on the run," he said, blinking back tears.

"I knew you were running from something … or someone," I whispered.

He sighed and turned his head to face mine. "Yeah, sure, I've been running. Who wouldn't want to leave that dump in the trailer park, hardly big enough for my mother, my younger brother, Nelson, and me. Soon as I was able to drive a rig, I lit out. I got a job driving trucks, and Nelson just smoked weed, waiting for lightning to strike. One day it did.

"I got into dealing with my brother and some sleazeball we called Snakeboots. He was a tall, grisly guy with bad teeth who showed up out of nowhere with stuff to sell when we were still trying to finish high school. That cowboy came up to us one night while we were getting high at the edge of the trailer park. 'Got a top-dollar job for you boys,' he said.

"It was a good job. Easy too. We just needed to get the product from A to Z. But the catch was the drop-off spot for the money. It was hidden, that's for sure. And nobody wanted to go there after dark. It was in the middle of the swamp—snakes, gators, king-sized mosquitoes and all."

The pieces of the circus boy's life were slowly interlocking in my mind. His circumstances were so far removed from my own I had been unable to even imagine them. "What about your mother? Didn't she worry about you going off to the swamp at night like that?" I asked.

West let out a long breath. "Momma just kicked back and lost it when Daddy left. She would shuffle around the trailer in dirty flip-flops, burn her fingers trying to light up old cigarette butts, and poke one eye down empty liquor bottles. For a while, we had to live on what we hunted; she was so gone. After I dropped out of high school, no one gave a shit if I came home to sleep or not. 'You're on your own now. Don't be leaning on me for nothing.' That was Momma's idea of making me a man. Sometimes I'd leave a box of day-old truck stop doughnuts on the kitchen counter in the trailer for Momma and Nelson before I'd light out again for another early morning haul. You know, I wanted things to be better for us. I really did."

I was listening with the bias of a lover, with an ear that would only retain the scenes of his life that I could dress up in glitter and romance. The rest—the drop-out living a dead-end life in a trailer was shut out, censored. That was not the West I had created for myself in my fantasies.

"Tell me about the swamp," I urged, hoping to rediscover the magical circus boy somewhere in his past. West turned over and propped himself up on one elbow to face me. His face softened; he was coming back to me, back to what I hoped was his true self.

"Out in the swamp, it was peaceful, no people making my life miserable with their bullshit and uppity crap. I was able to let everything in instead of tuning everything out. Most people I know, when they find themselves surrounded by nothing but light and green, they struggle with the peace, have to get stoned before they can slow down and read what is really going on. So much life happening all around.

"I took a machete and built a hut, cleared the ground, and laid down stones in a circle for my campfire. It was supposed to be my place to get away from my crap life, living on the edge of Florida's good times in Lake City with my do-nothing mother and shit-for-brains brother. I just didn't know I would end up living out there in the swamp on my own for almost two years."

"How did *that* happen?" I wanted to know.

"If I had to blame anyone besides myself, I would blame that asshole in the cowboy hat and snakeskin boots. His name was Randy, and maybe he *was* a horny motherfucker—my brother and I had a big hee-haw over that one. Nelson said shit like, 'He's such an ugly fuck, he can't be getting any!'" The circus boy relaxed on his back and cocked his arm over his forehead; he stared up at the metal crosshatched springs that held the mattress of the upper bunk.

"Why my brother and I fell in with that old-ass greaseball, I can't explain," he continued. "We were stupid, hungry, and all pie-eyed over all the money we were going to make in one go. And Randy had that confident, smooth talk and the black leather long coat and boots that were so badass that we made up our own name for the guy—Snakeboots. He was too cool, like the kind of guys we wanted to be when we got older."

"So you worked for that guy?"

"Yup."

"Doing *what*?" I asked.

"All I had to do was take a shipment of stuffed animals to Winter Park for the circus down there. Some of the teddy bears were loaded with dope; they had junk sewn into their hollow heads. The dolls—circus Barbies, we called them—carried the pills all rolled up in little squares of tin foil, like tiny joints, which were inserted between their legs, up their wazoos. Nelson laughed so hard that he sprayed his soda when we heard where the pills were hidden. Two years younger than me—he was such a kid. There were all kinds of drugs in the shipment: uppers and downers, even some LSD. I kept my eyes and ears open, trying figure out which toys carried what, just in case. I wasn't going to ask Randy, the king of shut-the-fuck-up-or-you're-dead."

"I can't believe no one ever stopped you—" I began, pausing to try to collect my thoughts. All this new information about West was dizzying.

"I picked up some serious skills," West boasted, "like how to smile wide and act all friendly while we loaded the boxes, telling jokes and glad-handing around with the clueless guys in the hangar. If there were drug-sniffing dogs, I had them follow me out into a field and gave them bits of truck stop beef jerky I'd filched from a jar at the checkout counter. Everyone in Florida was so easily distracted by a smile or a story. I got really friendly with the dogs too. It surprised me how easily I understood them and sensed what they were thinking. Because they were trained, they loved to work, to learn new things. I would make them do tricks, walk on their hind legs, jump through hula hoops and the like. It was another one of our ruses to make people believe we were with the circus."

I felt a wave of anxiety as I realized that many of West's circus talents overlapped with his previous life as a delinquent.

"Randy was impressed," West said and then imitated Snakeboots's Texas drawl, "'How you get them dogs to do all that stuff?' He told me it made me one of the best traffickers he'd ever worked with. So Snakeboots made me his partner and told my brother to go back to school till he could learn to tie his own shoes. Got to say, I was flattered."

"How did you get on the wrong side of that guy?"

"Randy decided we could go for an even bigger job, especially if I could get the drugs past the dogs. That day, we traveled for miles. At my last truck stop, I chatted up the cashier and slid twelve packs of beef jerky into my pockets while she sorted out the odd change I'd given her for my coffee to go. That day was fixing to be blue skies all the way."

"And? You got caught?"

"That same night after making the drop, Randy and I got totally wasted and took off joyriding in his car outside Deland. He was counting stacks of hundred dollar bills in a briefcase on his lap, like a fool, when we picked up blue lights flashing in the rearview."

As I lay there, quietly listening to the circus boy's deep voice with my head on his chest, I was struck by how far I had allowed my fantasies to unspool unchecked; my imagined West had never really existed. I wondered if I could still find a way to love the real West, the one who was opening up to me right now.

He continued his story uninterrupted, telling me they had been set up in a sting operation. The big drug deal gone right had gone totally wrong—a car chase, spike strips laid down by a police dragnet, a two-tire blowout, with the car rolling over and over down an embankment. West had crawled out of a broken window and started running furiously, blindly, through tears, blood, mucus, and an unspeakable pain in the ribs. He told me of the partner who didn't make it: Snakeboots. Maybe he got caught, or maybe he died from gunshot wounds. At the time, West didn't know. He only made his escape and never looked back.

He headed for the Seminole territories where he had learned to hunt with his father. Then, loaded with camping supplies, he disappeared into the Everglades. There, the struggle to stay alive took over. Time stretched from one day to the next. Over a year later, while hitchhiking his way to the Florida State border, he met up with the circus on a back road.

For me, the pieces began to fall into place—why West was so thin when he joined up with Reyes Bros. Ragtime Gypsy Show and why he'd spent months living in a Florida swamp on his own—as Red had said—like Tarzan. I had fallen in love with the story of a smooth-chested, strong young man, one who hunted and lived in untouched swamplands, learning stillness, hunger, and the absolute, wide-eyed alertness of the wild.

But then there was an asphalt intrusion erupting into view, spoiling my image of him. Hunger had led to helplessness, which led to hitchhiking and rolling with men in ditches for food or for a ride to the next town, the next break. West weighed next to nothing a year ago when he was picked up off the road by two drunken roustabouts, Wayne and Jesse. Wayne had traded sex with West in a filling station bathroom for a meal and a ride across the Florida state line. When Jesse found out the skinny young man could also drive a truck, he promised him a job at the circus. The job was smuggling drugs, same as before, but this time, West would have a shot at circus life too. He could stay on the move and hide out from the law.

And then, after a season of touring with the circus, it happened, the change—the tumble forward into the spotlight as the elephant trainer because of his uncanny ability to read animals and anticipate their thinking, their lust for survival. I had met West at the precise moment when he had succeeded in forging his new identity as a circus performer.

"And now you know things I hoped I'd never have to tell you." West sighed and slowly ran his fingers through my hair. "I don't have a lot of good things to give you, but whatever I have, it's yours. And you know my secrets. That brings you closer to me than my own blood."

If I had ever wanted to be loved deeply, here was a windfall. West had given me the chance to offer compassion, to bind the wound that threatened us both. I had achieved the intimacy I was after. Now there was a secret, a terrible one that only I knew. The lithe gyrations of the acrobatic twins would fail to wring my guts with envy. They would never know him as I did.

I opened my eyes and held his gaze. "Don't say I don't care about you. Because I do."

"Then there's no need to decide about the baby yet. What's the rush?" The circus boy placed a hand on my belly.

"I won't even be able to *get* an abortion if I'm too far along."

West winced, but he spoke gently. "You're thinking all the wrong thoughts, Sarah. Like, this baby is just a science experiment, and you're some kind of robot that can be tinkered with. There's a life inside you. And it's as much mine as it is yours. Remember that."

★ ★ ★

Hours later, while we were still lying in bed together, I heard Fritz's dogs barking furiously in the night and then howling in unison. West cloaked himself in his costume cape and stole out of the sleeper with a knife between his teeth. I grinned at his theatrical appearance, "You look like Zorro," I giggled.

"I'm going to see who's out there," he whispered.

I worried while he was gone, got up, and opened the sleeper door a crack. I lay in bed in the top bunk, trying to stay alert, listening for sounds of his return, but I fell asleep before he came back. Just before dawn, I woke up, suffering from bride's complaint—irritation from too much sex and no place to wash up afterward. West had returned to the sleeper. His naked body was stretched out on the bottom bunk: belly down, elbow crooked, hand under the pillow. *He's probably still holding the knife,* I thought.

Once outside, I found an inconspicuous spot to relieve myself at the edge of the woods where no one would see me. My skin tickled and burned when I peed. As I was zipping up, I was startled by the loud grinding creak of a metal sleeper door opening on rusty hinges farther down the midway. Someone else was up in the night too. On my way back, I looked across the lot and spied a man in a cowboy hat standing by the light truck where Jesse liked to bed down for the night under the chassis. From a distance, it looked as though there had been an oil leak under the truck, and the stranger was throwing hay on the spill. Jesse was nowhere in view. I crouched down in the weeds and waited for the cowboy to leave before creeping back to our sleeper.

NIGHT OF RIVER SECRETS

12

The next morning, when we were on our way to the cookhouse for our share of burned, oily coffee, Red came hobbling across the lot.

"Jesse has blown the show. Can't be found anywhere."

"Jesus, fuck!" West yelled. I detected fear in his eyes; the angry shouting was just for cover.

"What's wrong? What happened?" I asked, catching him at the bicep.

"Now I'll bet I have to do a double back and drive the light truck *and* the elephant truck to the next lot. *Shit!* Goddamn that bastard!" And he stormed off to protest to Lefèvre.

I didn't buy his charade. West was used to hard work. Something wasn't right. Red was left alone with me in the midway, and he waved me over and leaned into my ear to tell me a secret. "That ain't the half of it," Red hooted. "Wait till West finds out some crazy guy is looking for him."

The old man told me how he had been surprised in the night by a gentle tapping on the sleeper door of the office truck. Too tired to stand, Red had crawled on all fours and pushed the metal door halfway open in one half-hearted thrust. Suddenly the old canvas boss found himself staring at the end of a gun, pointed right at his face. Strangely, the man in a cowboy hat had

ELIZABETH CARTER WELLINGTON

withdrawn his weapon in disgust. "Guess I was too ugly to die," Red boasted to me.

We made our way through the ground fog to meet up with West and joined him at a table at the cookhouse. My bare elbows stuck to the tacky surface of the picnic table set up outside.

"Some roughneck came to the lot last night looking for you." Red leaned into West's shoulder. "You better figure out a way to keep him guessing. Tonight you and Sarah would be safer in the office truck if he thinks I'm sleeping there."

"So where are you going to sleep?" I asked while I pushed the last of my mealy grits around on my plate. By then, I was speaking all the time in a Southern accent. I liked the way the words came out all loosened up. It was irresistible.

"In the elephant truck. We'll swap." The old man picked up his fork and waved it at me. "But don't you go fixing up your bed special. I can bed down in the cab."

West narrowed his eyes and looked the old man in the face. "You sure you want to do this for me, Red? That guy can be one mean son of a bitch."

"Hell, he didn't kill me the first time! I hope he *does* drop by to see me at the elephant truck. He'll think I'm the Great Houdini!"

West put his hand on Red's shoulder and got up from the table without a word; he left us there, in a hurry to join the big top crew. Then Red and I walked together over to the office truck to get his things. He didn't have much. I carried his folding chair, and the old man slung a drab wool army blanket over one shoulder. We headed back to West's sleeper in the elephant truck. Something was going on. I trusted Red; I knew he could describe the guy who was looking for West and maybe even tell me why Jesse's departure had made West react with alarm.

"We're coming to the end of our run, so if anybody has got a problem with one of our men, they come looking for 'em now. Know what I mean?" Red explained.

"Kind of. Last night, West left the sleeper with a knife—for protection. Just beforehand, he told me about his past, about some jailbird he knew called Snakeboots. Do you think Snakeboots could be the same guy who pulled a gun on you?" I asked. I didn't mention that I had also seen a man in a cowboy hat prowling around Jesse's truck.

Red lowered his eyelids, lifted up his chin, and gave me a lofty look. "That'd be my guess. The best way to handle a snake is just to keep your distance. We're getting too close to where we picked up West in Florida. There's going to be some kind of altercation, one way or another."

"You sure? You really think that guy would come back?" I began to feel a tingling of apprehension.

Red raised his eyebrows and patted the cab door. "I always keep a gun on the floor of my truck. Got to have an emergency kit," he said. When he looked up to give me his wry smile, there was no twinkle in his eye.

★ ★ ★

We were coming to the end of our tour. For West, Florida was home, even though he had left this mother's trailer park as a teenager. When we reached our final destination in Deland, he would come full circle. I had traveled north to south, and I dreaded my return to cold, cantankerous New England, the ass backwards way of talking, always measuring everything in terms of what people were doing and not how they were feeling. Even flirtations never hit the mark. I could look forward to a winter of half conversations with bearded, bespectacled students who would approach me in Harvard Square and ask safe questions about the camera dangling from my shoulder. In the South, men weren't afraid to get right to it, "You got a boyfriend, sugar?"

Then there was the fact of my pregnancy. It was hard to believe because I didn't feel all that different—no morning sickness, no swollen belly popping out of my jeans. I had confided in

Margarita, and she was no stranger to a girl in trouble. "You stand against the stove at the cookhouse, or put a hot water bottle on your back, and maybe you get your period to come," suggested the Spanish woman as we sorted through the cardboard carton of circus toys back at her camper.

I didn't answer. Trying to induce a bloody miscarriage was too gruesome to think about. I didn't tell her that I had started taking vitamins that very morning. I turned my attention to our inventory. The little white fluffy dogs were selling out. We still had several big teddy bears left. I lifted one of them out of the carton.

"Why don't we find a way to sell these off, now we're out of Tennessee?" By then I'd guessed that she knew what I knew about "Grandpa" and the hundred-dollar bears. We had both silently agreed to look the other way. "Don't find trouble till trouble finds you" had been my motto.

The oversized head on the stuffed toy bear wobbled, and I lifted the red and yellow band of ribbon at the neck to check the stitching. A three-inch section at the base of the neck had been opened and sloppily sewn back up. The loose stitches made the head list to one side. I rummaged in the box for another bear, and its head almost came off in my hand. I took a quick peek inside; the hollow head was empty.

"Are all the bears like this one?" I showed the teddy bear to Margarita. The huge head hung down over its round belly. "The head on this one needs reattaching. No one is going to buy it like this."

I liked to position the big bear on the top of my stuffed animal pole and use it as a selling tactic. Having a big worker toy with a cute face on display was the key to selling my smaller stuffed animals. I often spoke in the bear's voice when talking to children, moving it around like a puppet. The older kids would laugh and say, "Do it again!" And the younger ones would stand stock still, entranced.

Margarita was aggravated. *"Ay Dios!* Jesse got into the last shipment, and he make a mess. Lefèvre tell me to sew them back up again, but I don't do this. I tell him, 'Sewing—how you say? Not my thing.'"

I was surprised, but I tried not to show it. I wondered if Jesse had taken all the dope and tried to make a run for it.

"Let me stitch them up, okay?" I scooped up the bears in my arms and nodded at Margarita with a smile over my shoulder as I left. While walking down the midway to get the sewing kit out of the bureau drawer in my sleeper, I passed by the ticket window of the office truck and caught sight of the ringmaster; he glanced up from his desk and straightened when he saw me. The office door opened, and Lefèvre stepped out; he intercepted me in front of the concession stand. "Where are you going with those?"

"To my trailer. They need mending." I held out one of the teddy bears. "See? The heads are wobbling all over the place."

"Give them to me," the Frenchman commanded, taking the bears out of my arms. "Sarah, this is not like sewing up the tent." His face was stern. "I want these bears mended by a professional seamstress—at the costume truck."

Lefèvre looked comical as he strode away, his rigid body upright in his tall black riding boots, carrying a pile of laughing oversized bears in both arms, as if they were children. One of the bear's heads bobbed and bounced up over his shoulder as he marched along.

★ ★ ★

Some say you can't step in the same river twice, and I'm telling you, it's true. The locals in Quitman will tell you to stay away from their river at night because they believe it to be haunted. I'm sure that's true too. We didn't mean for things to end up that way.

All West and I did was switch sleeper trucks with Red the night we reached Quitman, a beautiful old Georgia town, our last stop before we crossed back over the Florida line. The sleeper built into the office truck where Red slept was much larger than ours; it had a double bed instead of bunks. And because it housed the circus office and ticket window, the truck was always parked first in line, right next to the entrance marquee in the midway. The ringmaster never set foot in the office truck sleeper, which was reserved for the senior roustabout. Lefèvre and his daughters lived in a large mobile home on the performers' row. Red barely enjoyed his privileged sleeping quarters; he only used his bed when it rained. Because of his bad leg, crawling up into the truck cab and spending the night there was easier for him; he often stretched out on the bench seat with the windows rolled down.

West and I moved over to the office truck after dinner. I didn't even have to make up the bed; Red made sure I could bounce a penny on the tucked-in blanket—a habit from his circus days with the USO in Belgium.

After teardown, West and I settled down for the night. It was the first time we'd slept in a comfortable bed in a truck without animals—no thumping noises, no rocking back and forth—and we fell asleep listening to the sound of tree frogs by the river.

I was up in the night, as usual, looking for a place to pee at the edge of the woods. On the far end of the row of circus trucks that lined the midway, Red appeared to be awake in the cab of the elephant truck. Through the open cab window, I could see the old man sitting upright. He must have heard my footsteps approaching the woods.

He was muttering to himself. "Now who's prowling around out there?"

I finished my business quickly, and when I looked up from my hiding place in the woods, Red was pushing the passenger door open with one foot. He slipped out and down to the ground. I was sure the footsteps he'd heard had been mine. I was about to call out to Red, but he turned his back to me and moved in the direction of another figure in the shadows, lurking in the middle of the midway, close to the sideshow entrance. Through the gaps in the semitrailers, I made out the silhouette of a mangy-looking roughneck in cowboy boots, and something that looked like a silver belt buckle glinted in the moonlight.

It was Snakeboots. It had to be. I caught my breath. The cowboy had a gun in his hand. Huddled in the woods on the perimeter with the elephant truck in view, I froze in place and listened to the two men speak in low, aggressive tones.

"What the hell you want?" Red called out, limping over to face Snakeboots out in the midway.

"Mind your own goddamn business, old man." The cowboy came out of hiding and approached the wasted, bent body of the old circus bum with a careless disarticulated stride.

I moved closer to listen, taking care to stay hidden from view by staying behind the row of trucks in shadow along the edge of the trees until I came up behind the elephant truck. Red Maynard and the rough-hewn man now stood nose to nose in the midway; they were only a few feet away from the office truck where West was still sleeping. I flattened myself on the ground and crawled under the elephant truck to watch them.

"Where's that swamp rat? Tell me where he's at, or I'll blow your brains clear to Tallahassee." Snakeboots put a hand on his gun.

"Who gives a goddamn if you shoot me? Be fine with me to die any time." Red stood, swaying slightly. Their tense voices carried.

"Uh huh, big hero. Well, I'll find 'em myself. It won't bother you if I smoke both of 'em—West and his little girlie friend." He tipped his cowboy hat at Red. "Right, old man?"

I heard Snakeboots march down the midway in my direction, a flashlight beam swept under each of the painted trucks that lined the midway corridor. Snakeboots was searching for me too.

The sound of the cowboy's boots scuffling across the lot stopped and held still; Snakeboots was on the other side of my semitrailer. I could see the snakeskin tips of his boots pointing in my direction as I lay under the chassis. I heard an audible click, and light scattered in random flashes, like heat lightning, underneath the elephant truck. For a second, the flesh of my arms was illuminated. A shot of adrenaline flashed through my entire body as I scrambled backward out from underneath the chassis to stay out of view. I stood up, flattened myself against the semitrailer, and held a hand over my mouth, barely breathing through the nose, hoping Snakeboots hadn't seen or heard me.

Paralyzed, I didn't know what to do. If I went to warn West at the office truck, I'd lead Snakeboots right to him. If I moved a muscle, the cowboy would hear me and kill me. I stood stock still with my back pressed flat against the elephant truck in the shadow of the woods, wishing for some kind of noise to cover the sound of my frantic breathing.

Then Red started yelling, "Wake up, West! Snakeboots is here on the lot with an itchy finger! You better—" All of a sudden, Red's voice was cut off. I heard a thump as the cowboy brought his pistol down on Red's white head, and the old man crumpled softly to the ground without uttering another sound. As I peeked out through the gap between the container and the cab, I saw Red's legs collapse; he caved inward, like a house demolition, from the one blow to the brain.

"Yeah," hollered Snakeboots, "and I got your girlfriend!" I hopped back away from the cab toward the container. Light flickered by my ankles. It was too late. The roughneck had seen my feet underneath the trailer from his position on the other side of the elephant truck. Panicked, I made my feet disappear from view by hoisting myself up into the open container. I crawled in with the sleeping elephants.

Bessie and Mary were dreaming, standing up in their foot chains, heads bobbing, ears flapping gently. I felt around in the dark for a heavy tool to defend myself. There were training implements, along with a shovel and a muck rake hanging up on the interior wall. I ran my hands over them, recognizing the feel of the whip stock, until I laid my hands on the hot shot. I pulled the stun gun out of the clips that held it to the wall and turned it on.

A sudden crashing noise erupted several trucks down the line near the sideshow entrance. The cowboy's footsteps retreated; he was doubling back in the direction of the noise. I grabbed the hot shot and jumped out of the elephant trailer, shimmying over to hide behind the truck cab's passenger door. I inched my way up and huddled against the truck tire, peering around the corner of the battered fender to get a good look at the midway.

Red was on the ground, bleeding from the head. West burst out of the office trailer wearing only pants and ran straight for the woods. Snakeboots aimed and fired but missed and ran after him.

I jumped up and screamed "West, no!"

At the sound of my voice, Snakeboots wheeled around, changing course in an instant. He found me quivering in a T-shirt and underpants, backed up against the elephant truck. His boots crunched as he walked straight toward me, arm outstretched, gun pointed at my forehead.

"Okay then, one at a goddamn time." He smiled with malevolence, his long black leather coat hanging deadly silent around his ankles. He had a tooth missing and stank of sweat and booze. I gripped the hot shot with both hands and held my ground.

"Huh, like that's going to help you," he said. Snakeboots advanced on me, chuckling to himself. "You see, West?" he shouted over his shoulder in the direction of the woods. "This is what you get for running away in my hour of need."

I gave the man a wide-eyed look of astonishment.

"Oh yeah, sweetie pie," Snakeboots continued. "That piece of day-old shit can't be trusted at *all*. He just cut and run and left me holding. But guess what?" He leaned in close and held his pistol to my throat. I could smell the metallic odor of hunger under his whiskey breath as I shrank back against the side of the truck, the hot shot at my side.

"I found a way out of jail, and here I *am!* Ready to get back in business!" Suddenly the cowboy's free hand reached between my legs and cupped my pubic bone. He then stifled my scream by covering my lips with his filthy mouth. My head banged up hard against the truck wall.

Running toward us out of the dark woods, West hurled himself up on the man's back and gripped him from behind with his arms and legs; he flung his right forearm around the man's neck in a chokehold and began to squeeze with all his might. The cowboy lurched backward, still holding his gun, gagging and off balance. All at once, the gun in his hand went off, and a bullet tore through the trailer just above my head. The elephants inside the container trumpeted in fear, and the entire trailer began to pitch and sway as Bessie and Mary pulled at their foot chains. The cowboy began to fall backward, his whole torso displayed as he dropped his gun and raised his arms to pry himself loose from West's tightening grip.

Seizing the opportunity, I lunged at Snakeboots with the hot shot and struck him again and again with an electric charge to the chest, aiming for the heart. West jumped off the man's back as the electric shock penetrated Snakeboots's body. The cowboy's shoulders twitched violently; his legs buckled, and he fell to his knees, screaming. His whole torso shuddered and spun like a circus toy dangling from a stick before the yelling suddenly stopped and the cowboy pitched forward and fell face down to the ground. The roughneck's body lay in a heap at our feet.

"Run, Sarah. Go get Lefèvre!" West's voice cut though the haze, the crazy confusion.

Was he dead? Had I killed him? I scrambled under the elephant truck and hopped out the other side onto the midway concourse. Some of the trailers had lights on now. I ran to the performers' row and the village-like cluster of campers. Lefèvre's mobile home door opened, and the ringmaster stepped out, hurriedly shuffling his shoulders into a white frilly musketeer shirt with puffed sleeves. He gave me a short nod and then brushed past without a word. Lefèvre strode ahead of me along the midway in his black riding boots; I trailed behind at a trot in my bare feet. His face was set in a grim expression, like a wax death mask. One by one, the lights in the campers went out; shades were pulled back down and curtains drawn. Lefèvre would handle any ruckus caused by lowlife roustabouts. Everyone at the circus operated under the assumption that they were better off not knowing too much.

The ringmaster attended to Red first. I was relieved to see that the old man had regained consciousness. Lefèvre asked me to help him load Red's frail body into the cab of the office truck, and we did our best to make him comfortable. The old man waved me off when I grabbed a sweat rag from the dashboard and pressed it to his head wound. "Nothing to worry about, little sister, it's just a flesh wound." Red smiled weakly, "Go on and skedaddle."

"Where is the intruder now?" Lefèvre's voice was stern.

"Back at the elephant truck," I said.

When we reached the spot, the scene had not changed. West hovered over the body of the fallen cowboy, with the bowie knife gripped in one hand. Then the ringmaster spoke to me in his steely French accent: "You go back to bed in your own sleeper, and let Red rest at the office truck. And stay out of sight. I don't want you to be seen here." His voice was low and controlled, the voice he used to command the big cats in the ring.

I hopped back up into our sleeper in the elephant truck immediately and shut the door, leaving it open a crack to spy on the scene of the two men in the moonlight. They turned Snakeboots over on his back. With relief, I could see the silver belt buckle at the cowboy's waist moving up and down. He was unconscious but still breathing.

West crouched down quietly next to the sprawled body of the drug dealer who had once been his partner. Lefèvre looked up at the open crack in my sleeper door; he must have known I was watching. Then, in a brisk movement, the ringmaster sat on his heels and took the fallen man's pulse at the gland under the chin and then at the wrist. He locked eyes with West and murmured something I couldn't hear as the cowboy's limp hand fell away, settling in a clutch of fingers in the dirt. Then Lefèvre slowly stood up, looked gravely at West again, and shook his head from side to side. I suspected the ringmaster was performing this bit of theater for my benefit, but it was hard to tell in the dark.

"Is he dead?" I called through the metal door of our sleeper.

Through the crack in the door, I saw the ringmaster jerk his head in my direction, urging West to say something to me. The elephant trainer pressed his knees and stood up, and I hopped back, away from the door. The circus boy climbed up into our sleeper, and I busied myself adjusting the flame of the kerosene lamp on the dresser.

West looked at me with tired eyes, "It's all right, Sarah," he said in a hoarse whisper. "You killed him." His eyes shone with a false sparkle in the dim light. West had kept secrets, but he had never lied to me before. That glittery look was for conning townies. With rising indignation, I suspected he was lying to me now.

"*I* killed him? Wait a minute; are you sure?" I wanted to jump down to the ground to see for myself, but West blocked my way. He held me by the wrist at the sleeper door.

"West, what are you …?" I shuddered in disbelief. "I'll be tried for murder!"

"Killing to save a life isn't murder, Sarah," he murmured into my hair as he pulled me close into an embrace. "You did a good thing. Snakeboots was just some riffraff nobody is going to miss." West released me and pushed me down on the bed playfully with his fingertips and lay down on top of me. "You're alive. I'm alive. You should be glad." He kissed me, pressing the length of his body close. He was hard. Like a wrought iron tent stake. "You've got to be quiet about this whole thing, understand?" He pushed himself off me, grabbed up a tool satchel from under the bunk, threw it out the sleeper door, and followed it by leaping down to the ground.

"Jesus, West. What are … you going to do?" I stammered.

"Get rid of him. What do you think?" He turned and gave me a dark look. "Listen, don't you *ever* ask me about Snakeboots again, you got that? This is the last you'll ever hear of him. He doesn't exist. Never did."

Then I saw them take the cowboy's body by the hands and feet and drag it into the woods. In the darkness, I lost them from view, but I managed to make out the shining blade of West's bowie knife in the ringmaster's hand.

Determined to find out if Snakeboots was really dead, I followed them into the woods, stepping with as much stealth as I could, trying not to snap sticks and turn over rocks. I concealed my body in West's costume cape and shadowed the two men at a distance as they made their way to the river. The roar of the rushing water almost drowned out the sound of the cowboy's muffled screams while West held the man down and Lefèvre slit his throat.

They had lied to me. I hadn't killed Snakeboots at all, but I knew I'd helped out by jabbing him with the hot shot. At that moment, I wished somehow it wasn't true, that I hadn't seen West wash the blade of his knife in the river and then chuck it into the weeds before bending over in the darkness to pick up his shovel.

I crept out of the woods—picking my way through the leaves and low branches as quickly as possible—and ran back to the sleeper. I threw the cape in the bureau drawer and then crawled up into the truck cab to wait.

When the ringmaster and West returned, sullen and exhausted, they told me they'd dumped the body of the dead man in the river.

"Made sure to bury the snakeskin boots though," West assured me with a grimace, shifting the tool satchel from his shoulder to the ground, "Got to make it hard to ID a drowned man."

"You take the bed," I said stonily through the open cab window. "I can't sleep."

"Fine," said West, and he threw the bag of tools up into the sleeper, hopped up, and closed the metal door.

AT THE MOVIES

13

Stumbling around in the woods at dawn the following morning while West slept, I searched for the mound of fresh dirt where he'd buried the boots. If I found the spot, then maybe I could find the bowie knife close by too. *No one was going to stick me with a murder charge.* I was seething with outrage.

Not far from the river, the grasses became marshy, and my bare feet sank into a slick pool of slime. I staggered. My feet made a sucking sound when I lifted them out of the muck, and a thin rim with a reddish tint now lined the tops of my ankles. I had accidentally stepped into the dead man's pool of blood. My stomach turned, and I tried to vomit, but I could only double over, retching in dry heaves as I waded into the river. I was desperate to wash off the sticky red goo. I willed myself to leave the river and return to the circus grounds, taking a long route through the trees, away from the murder site.

Birdsong began to fill the air. On the lot, all was peaceful in the stillness of another early morning. It was strange to see the circus at rest at this hour. Roustabouts were sleeping in for the first time since they'd left winter quarters the previous spring. The jump to our next lot in Lake City was only seventy-seven miles away according to our route card.

I walked zombie-like out of the woods and approached the

open container where the elephants were awake, bobbing their rounded Indian elephant heads and creaking happily at seeing me. Bessie reached out her trunk and wrapped it around my waist, gently this time, and I hugged her back, wrapping my arms around her trunk and leaning my cheek against her warm, leathery hide. I was convinced these animals could sense the truth, the things that West and Lefèvre wouldn't admit to themselves or to me. West had saved my life; yet he wanted me to believe I was responsible for a murder I didn't commit. Head throbbing, I curled up in the hay at the far end of the trailer. It was the only place I felt safe.

When morning broke, a hot Georgia sun warmed my knees as I sat mute in the open container door with my feet hanging down, staring into the woods. I wanted to leave that lot right away, but I didn't want to pretend the killing hadn't happened. A man was dead, and his death had been partly my fault. I wanted to punish myself by knowing this truth, by looking at it straight on.

After that night of river secrets in Quitman, I just couldn't stay on with West. I kept hearing the bullet crack into the metal over my head; my guts seized at the thought. Something cold had entered my body right in the place between my legs where pleasure had been. I realized that I was planning to take another life, an innocent one this time—the unwanted child I was carrying.

West was free from Snakeboots, and now, he would be free of me too. That day, I could feel the cold in everything we did. We shared relief, the thank-God-we're-alive type of relief, but the horror of what had happened would keep our eyes from meeting. Being around a dead man had sickened my soul, even though I'd been five inches from trading places with him.

West approached me just as the trucks were getting ready to leave. "It's over, Sarah," he said with the slightest hint of irritation.

"What's over?" I startled when I heard his voice. I had been in a deep fog.

"He's gone," West explained quietly. "There's no need to be afraid now. Besides, we got to move on."

Moving on. It was so easy for him, I thought.

"Snakeboots may be gone, but it's not over," I said, my voice a monotone. "What happened last night will never be over. Not for me." I stared ahead into the woods with a blank expression. Rivers hold many secrets, and now I knew that some of those secrets could be traced back to a life on the run.

"Listen to me, Sarah. Here at the circus we make our own rules—mete out justice on our own terms. We're a little society apart, with our own codes and laws." I shook my head slowly back and forth, unable to understand.

"You saw how we got rid of the water boy when he crossed the line," West offered.

"What about Jesse?" I asked.

"What about him?" West responded, leaning forward suddenly with intense interest.

"Someone murdered him," I whispered. "I'm sure of it."

"Well, we can't protect everyone from the trouble they're running from. Sometimes someone from the outside breaks through."

"I think Snakeboots killed Jesse," I said, fear rising in my voice.

"What makes you say that?" asked West.

"When I got up in the night back in Warner Robbins, I saw a man with a long coat and cowboy hat leaning over, throwing hay down on a big pool of oil under Jesse's truck. The next day Jesse was missing."

"Why didn't you tell me? Jesus, Sarah!"

I shrank back into the truck container, pulled my knees to my chest, and hugged them close. My head fell forward and I began to cry, "I didn't know—"

The circus boy jostled my shoulder gently. "Hey, you know we can't stay here. You'll feel better once we give it some distance. You're a real circus girl now, Sarah," said West in an attempt to bring me back. "You have a dark shadow in your past to run from now. Just like me." He put his arm around me, and I struggled not to reveal how much I feared him, hoping he would believe I had gone rigid for other reasons. By then, I had plenty of them.

West broke the heavy silence that had sprung up between us. "Lefèvre wants to see you over at the office truck before we hit the road."

"He wants to see *me*?"

"Yeah." West was giving me nothing. "Just knock before you go in."

★ ★ ★

The summoning frightened me even more. I had never entered the office truck before, not even when I'd had my chance to ride with his daughter, Brigitte. Any business with the ringmaster was always conducted in the open on the midway or through the ticket window.

When I got there, the ticket window was closed, but I could hear the rustle of movement inside the trailer. I waited a moment on the folding metal steps and then rapped softly. Lefèvre opened the door, nodded to the chair in front of his desk, and I stepped in. He sat like an aging king, surrounded by images of his glory days on the Clyde Beatty Show. Circus posters and framed black-and-white photographs of lions and tigers in various poses covered every inch of the wall behind him. In the center was a large autographed photo of a grinning Clyde, Lefèvre, and a couple of Hollywood celebrities I couldn't place.

The ringmaster rested his elbows on the desk, tented his fingers, and waited for my eyes to finish absorbing the images of his personal hall of fame. I could see that this atmosphere was meant to impress. Lefèvre was handling me.

He cleared his throat just as I caught sight of the three damaged teddy bears he had taken away from me. They were bundled up in a garbage bag, thrown into a corner behind a file cabinet. I faced the ringmaster. The man was all business—nothing in his demeanor indicated he had participated in a murder the night before.

"I have a new job for you," he declared pleasantly. "Bessie stepped on Serpentina's foot in practice." When my eyebrows shot up, the ringmaster hurried to explain, "She's fine, but she has to wear a brace on her foot. My daughter, Celeste, will perform with the elephants in Serpentina's place. But we need an extra bally girl on hand, just in case, to style and hand props to the performers." The smile beneath his thinning moustache was tight and fleeting.

I was immediately suspicious. I had barely managed to scratch out a place on the payroll as a member of the setup crew, and now I was being promoted to bally girl? "I'm sorry I have to ask, but is that the real reason?"

Lefèvre dropped his chin onto the little bridge he made with interlaced fingers and leveled his gaze at me, "Well, maybe yes, maybe no."

"Uh huh," I prodded.

"You are a very beautiful young lady, and your promotion to bally girl should not surprise you."

I was not taken in by the Frenchman's flattery. I could see that whatever was at stake mattered a great deal to him. "But it does surprise me," I insisted.

He centered his shrewd gray eyes on my face, "We are having trouble with the police." His expression clouded over, and I sensed he was about to bring out the knife. "It seems you have attracted their attention … by rolling around under the trucks with the roustabouts! You have made us such a spectacle of disrepute that some God-fearing do-gooder alerted the cops! I had the police in my office for an hour asking me if you were a teenage runaway—"

"I'm not—"

"*Tais-toi!*" He held up his hand in annoyance. Then he let out a sigh of exasperation and continued, "Don't worry, I defended you, but I had to make up a story. First, I tell them the truth; you are an incorrigible tomboy." He smiled, tight-lipped, and shook his head from side to side. "*Mon Dieu*, I pulled you out from under the truck myself! Second: I explain your silly behavior with West. I say that all that tickling and laughing is innocent—*complètement*—because although it may appear otherwise ..." the ringmaster paused for effect, "you are brother and sister."

"What?" I burst out.

The ringmaster closed his eyes, his mouth set in a tense, thin line as he waited to continue his speech uninterrupted. "I told the police that young people—even minors—perform in the circus all the time but that they join the show with their families. I vouched for you and West; I told them you had grown up together in the circus as children of circus stars."

I sat there in disbelief. "And I have to perform—"

"Not perform. But you must dress in costume during the show—you know," he waved his hand at the wrist in small circles. "Look like a bally girl."

"When?"

"Tomorrow afternoon. Our last show in Deland. The police will be coming to the circus to check my story. *Sans doute*. After the unfortunate events of last night, I think it would be wise not to give the police any reason to stick their noses under the tent, so to speak." He made a funny face by elongating his features and pretended to lift up a tent flap with two fingers. I laughed agreeably on cue. This was the first time the ringmaster had tried to charm me.

My relief was palpable. When I left his trailer, I felt a trickle of sweat run down my side. The underarms of my peasant blouse were soaked through.

★ ★ ★

Two more days with the traveling show—today in Lake City and tomorrow in Deland—and I could collect my pay in cash from Brigitte at the ticket window in the office truck and head to the airport in Orlando. If I wanted to cash out, I would have to ride with the circus until we reached winter quarters in Deland. Withholding pay was the way the ringmaster bought loyalty and kept as many hands on staff as possible until the tour was over. I had saved up about two hundred dollars in the circus bank, enough to buy myself a ticket to New York La Guardia airport and pay for an abortion.

I didn't have it all figured out, but I knew I could crash at an older girlfriend's place once I got to New York. Abortions were illegal in Massachusetts, but I'd heard that a pregnancy counseling underground could help me get into a clinic in New York City. It would be my only chance to terminate the pregnancy before I reached ten weeks. By then, it would be too late, and I would be refused, even at the clinic in Manhattan. Costs were adding up. I would have to take a bus back home to Boston from New York after it was all over.

West was waiting for me in the elephant truck, motor rumbling. I jumped obediently into the cab, propped my head in the open window, and watched images of Quitman and "the unfortunate events of last night" recede in the rear view mirror. We didn't say a word to each other until we had left Georgia far behind.

One thing I really liked about crossing the border into Florida was the orange juice. The weigh station officials handed out little Dixie cups of fresh-squeezed orange juice to all the roustabouts who stopped their circus rigs. There was nothing to worry about at the weigh station at the state border. Florida was home to so many circuses that they took bribe money and let us pass through with a tip of a hat and a friendly wave. West brought an extra cup of juice out to me as I sat up in the cab, waiting our turn to drive onto the scale to pay our "fine."

The pleasure divined from that sweet-sour taste hit my senses like a drug. Noticing my rapture, West took the trouble to go inside the weigh station to ask for more. When he emerged, he was careful not to spill a drop on his way back over to the truck.

Peering into my face, as if asking for approval, West handed me a second cup with a wide smile. "You sure like it, don't you?"

I held his offering in both hands, like an addict, wondering if this sudden interest in orange juice was a pregnancy craving or a joyful reunion with food that wasn't fake or canned.

As the truck hummed along, I began to relax. Then my head dropped, and I fell asleep. When I woke up, I felt different. My mood had lifted. I looked at West, who was driving with one wrist cocked over the wheel. He must have noticed the change in my expression. He glanced over and smiled at me, "Feeling better now?" he asked.

"Yeah," I said, almost in disbelief.

"What did Lefèvre want to talk about?"

"Oh! You won't believe this, West!" I surprised myself by giving in to a cascade of helpless laughter, and when I caught my breath, I described my meeting with the ringmaster in glorious detail, animating every exchange. I was perhaps too caught up in my own theater to notice that West wasn't laughing along with me.

"You're going to like this one," I said, giddy with anticipation of West's reaction. "We have to pretend that we're brother and sister!"

"What? What the hell for?"

"Yeah, crazy, right? He says the police have got their eyes on me."

"Oh yeah?"

"Yeah, it's all because the cops saw me resting under the truck with you. They think I'm a teenage runaway or something."

"Yeah," said West. He took a deep breath and blew it out between his lips in a soft whistle. "I get it." We rode for several minutes in silence. Conversation resumed as soon as we started seeing placards with red arrows.

"He didn't ask you anything else?" West wanted to know.

"Who?" I asked, momentarily lost. What had I been talking about?

"Lefèvre. Did he ask you any questions?" West persisted.

"Not really. Why? Are *you* worried that I can't pass myself off as a bally girl?"

"Nah," said West, taking my hand across the seat. "You'll be great."

★ ★ ★

When we arrived in Lake City, the ringmaster invited the whole ensemble, cast and crew, to the movies—a Western—a rare afternoon off before our final performances of the season. Performers and roustabouts filled the entire movie theater.

"Hey!" Deuce called out behind me in the theater when the image of a toothless man with a wandering eye filled up the movie screen. "That looks like Shorty's brother!" The circus audience laughed and clapped in unison at the young hero on screen who was thrown from a horse.

"Try riding them backward and sideways!" someone called out. Other roustabouts joined in, shouting out from their seats. By the time West arrived, all the seats were taken in my row. Margarita sat to my right, and the acrobat twins sat to my left, which was fine with me because West and I had to act as if we were brother and sister anyway. He sat down in the seat directly behind mine and handed me a large soda cup of fresh orange juice and crushed ice. I relished its cold, sweet taste and sucked on the straw until it gurgled, grinning foolishly as I recalled how my mother would rebuke me for making "hoggish noises" in public.

I fell into the glazed-eye thrall of movie watching for some time—thirty minutes or more. I felt my body relax completely, as if I were melting like taffy on a sidewalk. My knees fell apart, and my fingers let go as my body sprawled in my seat, unaware of its usual boundaries. Then the cup slipped from my hands, and ice chips scattered at my feet.

"Are you all right?" It was Margarita. In an attempt to pick up my soda cup, I had pitched over suddenly to one side and jostled her arm, spilling the box of popcorn in her hand. I looked at Margarita, and her heavily made-up face became elastic. It morphed and changed expression in exaggerated ways like a cartoon imprint on silly putty. I opened my mouth to speak and found that my throat had been taken over by an attack of giggles.

Then the whole theater exploded into laughter. I saw their mouths open, their bodies rock forward, and their earrings sway. A strange subterranean light reflected off the white smiles of the performers seated next to me. In that moment, their faces in profile looked so beautiful in the darkness that I forgot why they were laughing. But I was laughing too—so hard that I lost my bearings and forgot where I was. I became breathless and began gasping for air, bent over double, my racing heart thumping in my chest. Was I going to die laughing? This thought set off another round of uncontrollable giddiness.

"You see, Sarah? Everything's going to be all right," said West from the seat behind mine. I felt him place a hand on my shoulder. Suddenly my perception about where I was changed completely. West's touch made me jump. His hand became the insistent, heavy paw of the male tiger, laying claim to the female. I shot out of my seat and stumbled into the aisle.

In my mind, I was in the Colosseum. The roar of the crowd vibrated through me, and I searched for familiar faces. With horror, I recognized Snakeboots in the back row. He stood up and waved the hotshot. I ducked down on all fours in the aisle and found myself desperately trying to crawl up the velvet carpeting on the theater stairs, terrified and repulsed by the blood stains that oozed out of the plush pile of the carpet wherever I placed my hands.

Later I was told that Margarita and Alana had hustled me out of the theater and into the ladies room, where I vomited before slumping to the floor. When I came to my senses, Margarita stood alone next to me. I was kneeling on the bathroom stall floor, transfixed by the mosaic of tiny, hexagonal, white tiles. I traced their edges with one finger. Everything around me seemed so bright and white in a monochromatic way. *Overexposed*, I thought, and then I rested my head on my elbows. I was breathing easily, staring down into the cool rushing water at the bottom of a toilet bowl. I embraced it, hung my head, and felt immense relief and joy at my return to sanity.

"Come on, Sarah," said the Spanish woman who crouched next to me in platform shoes. She helped me to my feet with steady arms.

I grimaced and slowly got up to rinse the sour taste of vomit out of my mouth at the sink. I looked at Margarita in the mirror and said, "I think West put something in my drink."

"Don't talk crazy! Why he want to do that, honey? He know you're pregnant. Everybody know."

"But I told him I don't want to keep it. Everything is so messed up," I said wearily.

"Don't worry." Margarita patted my shoulder. "I make you good soup tonight. We make you better."

Fighting waves of nausea, I wandered out into the lobby with my head held erect to avoid looking down at the dizzying design on the fake oriental carpet. West was waiting for me at the theater exit, and I nodded to Margarita. I wanted to have it out with him alone.

"You spiked my drink, didn't you?"

West looked at me with a kind of helpless sorrow in his eyes.

"Why would you do that to me?" I asked, clenching my teeth, determined not to cry in public.

He looked at the ground and said quietly, "You have no idea what you're up against. Don't you see? I'm trying to keep you from saying something crazy and getting us all in a heap of trouble. Lefèvre has got to think you don't know anything, that you're just some hippie airhead that wandered onto the lot."

"You couldn't just ask me to fake it? After all we've been through?" A blanket of depression rolled in like morning fog and settled over my senses. I was very, very sad.

"Not with a circus veteran like Lefèvre. He can see through every mask there is." West's face was grim. "I am so sorry," he pleaded, but I shied away when he reached for my hand.

"And I didn't kill *anyone*." I challenged him in an angry whisper. "Why put the blame on me? Why would you want to make me live with that burden all my life?"

The circus boy let out a breath and shuffled his feet. "You can't go talking to the cops about what you saw. Snakeboots was ready to kill you, just like he killed Jesse. He's that fucked up, just one big ball of rage. But it's okay now. He's gone. And it makes perfect sense for a girl like you to fight off a rapist, kill him by accident in self-defense, and then go a little crazy in the head. That's not the kind of story that sends someone to jail, not down here."

"But that's not what happened," I whispered, watching the others exit. And still clenching my teeth, I pretended to smile.

"What *difference* does it make? It's the story we need, and it's the story we'll tell if we have to. You got it? I'm just trying to protect you from something much worse."

"Oh shit, like *what*?" I protested and then added under my breath, "What's worse than a murder charge?"

He leaned into my ear and spoke softly, "Getting killed in a circus accident. Happens all the time." I saw the circus boy's eyes darken as he drew away from me.

"I don't like this at all, West. I don't think I can be with you right now," I said. The circus people gave us a wide berth as they streamed out of the theater. They must think we're having a lover's quarrel, I thought.

"You think *I* like this?" West was indignant. "Please, Sarah. Just play along. And stay away from Lefèvre. Don't let him ask you any questions. The hardest thing you'll have to do is sit tight until our last day. Once we both cash out, we're home-free. If the ringmaster suspects, for even a second, that you know something, Sarah, he will come for you, believe me. He is one ruthless motherfucker."

I stepped back and looked at him in horror. My head was spinning.

"You think that being with me puts you in danger, but it doesn't." West moved closer until we were side by side, arms barely touching. He lowered his voice and spoke to the floor. "It's just the opposite; I'm your protection." The shock of dark hair fell in across his face; after a moment, I turned to him and smoothed it back.

"Is that it?" I asked. "No more skeletons in *your* closet I don't know about?"

"Nah, there's nothing you don't know about me. I made one big mistake, and I ran away from it as far as I could go. Hell, I went all the way up to New England and back. And I found you."

"So no more life on the run? No more shady deals?"

"It's over, Sarah. Really."

"Promise?" I asked.

"You have my word," he said. "That whole chapter of my life is over. I'm free now. Finally."

The circus boy was thoughtful; his eyes drifted beyond the cars in front of the theater to the horizon. "Let's get out of here," he said suddenly.

"And go *where*?"

"To visit my family in Lake City."

"What? Now?"

"Yeah, why not? There's still time. We only have the one show to perform tonight."

★ ★ ★

As we left the circus grounds, it was hard to ignore the fact that the tour with the Reyes Bros. Ragtime Gypsy Show was coming to an end. We were headed back to life in the real world. The rows of track housing in the distance and strip malls stood out against the sky, trashing the sweep of green. I felt more disoriented with every step we took toward the city. The thought of leaving the circus was stalking my senses. I tensed up inside, anxiously bracing for the loss. I took West's hand; I needed someone to hold on to.

West let out a sigh. "We're going to be coming into winter quarters in a couple of days," he mused. *And then, God only knows what's going to happen after that,* I thought.

"Yeah," I said absently, thinking about what the hell I was going to do. I was no longer so sure about getting an abortion. Each day that passed brought me closer to the realization that I was carrying a child as my breasts grew tender, and my moods became more and more volatile. My pregnancy was real to me now.

"I'm thinking about keeping the baby, West," I said quietly. We walked on for several minutes without exchanging another word. West's loose grip on my hand tightened slightly. I was surprised that West, always so talkative, was holding out on me. I had expected him to jump for joy, say *something.* But we kept walking and walking until we reached the edge of an uncut field where wild flowers were growing in abundance.

West slowed his pace and turned to me. "Be my wife," he declared.

"Be your wife?" I repeated, taken aback.

"We'll elope," suggested West.

"Oh my God," I said without enthusiasm. I was too shocked.

"What do you say, why not?"

"I don't think I can do something like that without telling my parents," I said. Still, giddiness was bubbling up inside me.

"You make it easy to forget you're only seventeen." West smiled, "Call your parents. Tell them." He took my hand and pulled me along until we were running through the field in search of the nearest phone booth. I began to laugh with a mix of hysteria and abandon. This feeling of pure delight reminded me of those long-ago evenings of my childhood when the cows broke through the barbed wire fence. I gave in to the thrill of everything going so radically out of control. Married! Just like that.

Before we reached an asphalt road to follow into town, the circus boy paused, snapped off a handful of Queen Anne's Lace growing along the edge of the field, and got down on one knee. I bit my lip and smiled down at him, trying to catch my breath.

He looked up at me with his golden brown eyes shining. "Miss Sarah, I would be honored if you would be my bride. Will you accept me as your husband?" I was not at all prepared for a formal marriage proposal.

"What do you want me to say? Can't I think about it?"

"Think? That's the last thing you should be doing. What are your feelings for me, goddammit! Has your fancy upbringing brainwashed you, so you don't even know how you feel?"

"How about I put you on my list of interested suitors," I said coyly, bowing away from him.

"Don't play with me now, Sarah. I'm down here on my knees. This is serious." West was motionless as a cat ready to spring, and his eyes never left my face.

"How can you be so sure this is going to work?" I knew I was coming at the problem from different angles and was just making things worse by playing for time.

"Because I believe in us. God brought us together and made us a child, a child I thought I could never have.

"That's it. That's the real reason. You don't love me as much as you think. You just want me to have your baby."

"You don't get it at all, do you? What the hell do I have to do to prove to you I love you, I've always loved you, and I always will?" West got up off the ground and pressed the flowers into my hands. He stood so close I could feel the heat coming off his chest.

"Nothing," I said, serious at last. "You saved my life; that's enough."

"I'm not asking you to marry me because you owe me. I'm asking you because I think we have a chance."

"But we come from such different backgrounds, West." I faced him down with the truth, but he reacted with calm.

"That we do. And yet we're still so much alike. I've never met anyone with a hunger for life like yours. Now I could choose to think of you as a socialite, a Boston snob, or whatever, and you could think of me as your fling with some low-class guy. Slumming, they call it. Just a pinch in your ass before you go back to your nice little life.

"But who's to say we can't ditch the roles they want us to play? I am *not* some low-class guy without chances. I've *got* chances; I've taken them. And I'm willing to take a gamble and risk the worst kind of heartbreak just to spend my life with you by my side. I *know* we can be something together. There's a spark, some untamed part inside both of us that brings us together, and we've got to stay that way, make them all sick with envy for what it is that sets us apart. Lovers. Forever."

West began to pace back and forth, punctuating his speech with emphatic hand gestures. "You can decide to see me as some delinquent, or you can see me as the man I have always been. *You* know who I am behind all the gossip, all the *lies* and bad raps. You and my beautiful girls, Bessie and Mary. So don't go imagining me to be anyone else; I haven't changed at all. You're the one for me, and I'm the one for you. That's it."

We stood there in silence for a moment, facing each other, hands by our sides.

"Okay," I said.

"Okay, *what?*" the circus boy pressed gently.

"Okay, I'll make the phone call," I confirmed.

West gathered me in his arms and held me close for several minutes. I saw that tears were streaming down his face when we came apart. The tenderness of his movements as he pushed my hair back off my collarbone moved me to tears as well. We linked hands and resumed walking to town to call my parents. *I was going to need some protection out in the big wide world*, I thought to myself. *Why not West?*

At a pay phone at the first gas station we came to, I made the wedding announcement in a backhanded way, testing the waters for my parents' reaction. "West, the elephant trainer, has asked me to marry him." I made a point of excluding my response to his offer.

My mother's voice rang out brightly over the phone, "Sarah, honey. I am so *happy* for you!" she cooed.

My father came to the phone. I could hear ice clinking in his glass. "Congratulations, darling," he said fluidly. He was tipsy.

"Thanks, Dad."

"So!" he said with good cheer, as if making a toast at an office party, "We're finally getting *rid* of you!" There was a roar of laughter from those assembled. He went on, determined to land one more joke at my expense. "Now you'll stop running around like a *bitch in heat!*" The hilarity among the well-heeled men reached its peak. I wondered if they all shared a desperate camaraderie, having lost control of their wives and daughters.

"Stanwood!" I heard my mother bristle at my father. There was a brief muttering, and then she was back on the line. "Sarah? Hello?"

I was still reeling. My father's attack had cut me in half. I was left speechless. I held the receiver in my hand, shaking with anger. "I'm here." I was defiant, ready to throw down the phone.

"Don't hang up, honey. Your father is just … you know … I'll ask him to wire two plane tickets to the American Express office in Orlando tomorrow. We want to meet the gentleman who captured your heart." There was a pause as I considered this. I could hear the chatter of party guests in the background.

"I don't know …" The conversation couldn't accommodate long pauses, and I became aware that it was no longer private. There were too many merrymakers in the background vying for my mother's attention, and her vivacity must have drawn a little crowd around her. I could hear the jostling and whispering of her lady friends in cocktail dresses in the background and loud snickers from their husbands. "Another bachelor bites the dust!" one of them crowed. "Hear! Hear!"

"Nonsense," my mother insisted, keeping a firm grip on the reins of the conversation. "Your father and I can't wait to make plans. Leave it to you—the youngest—to be the first to get married!" She turned away from the phone to call out the kitchen window when she said it to make my engagement known to the party-goers. I could easily imagine the terrace setting of the cocktail party, under the leafy copper awning of the ancient beech tree I had climbed as a child. My mother would be wearing rouge and lipstick that left a bright red mark on the cigarette she would leave to burn itself out in a glass ashtray from Shreve's. She would be wearing her sleeveless dress, a sheath of black polka dots on white silk that set off her womanly shape, a mother of four. I could hear her movie star smile bleeding through every word when she said, "We'll be waiting for you and your young man with bells on!"

"Okay. But *please* tell Dad not to send any tickets. I've got my own money. I can pay for my own airfare … to come home." A lump rose in my throat. I lost my voice for a moment, the cry that would not come. I still hadn't decided where I would be going first, to New York or Boston.

"Sarah …? Are you still there?"

I took a deep breath, determined to save face, "Sure, everything's fine, Mom. I was just looking for my route card to give you a date. I'll get paid after the show ends around October seventeenth—"

"Is your beau there with you? Put him on—"

"No, Mom. He's back in the ring, practicing with the elephants. And I've got to go now and join him. I'm going to be in the show!" I said, bending the truth, as usual.

"Well, tell him how pleased we are. This is *such* a surprise. Wonderful news! Just marvelous!" I was amazed at how quickly she had accepted the news of the proposal. But before she could shower me with any more superlatives, I ended the call.

"Okay, Mom. I've got to go. I'll see you soon."

"We love you, Sarah," she said.

"Love you too," I said clearly, but my voice broke at the end. I hung up the greasy receiver in a hurry, before the tears came. I stood with my hand over my mouth trying to stifle a sob, steadying myself with my shoulders against the glass wall of the phone booth. West came over at once, concerned.

"It's all right, West. You have their blessing," I said. "I guess that's what you call it. It's just that they embarrassed me in front of all their country club friends. My father called me a bitch in heat."

"Oh hell, Sarah. Fuck 'em. Don't you *ever* worry about what anybody thinks, remember?" West assured me, wrapping my shoulders with his flak jacket.

"You're right about that. *Fuck* 'em." I yelled, and I felt better. West always seemed to be able to get my little boat to rights whenever it was sinking.

I hadn't expected my parents to approve of the marriage. I couldn't believe it. Judging from our brief exchange, my father rightly suspected I was no longer a virgin. I was just another young flower child caught up in the romance of the times. But it had never occurred to me until then that, in my parents' world view, sex had to be sanctioned by marriage. Love. Marriage. Sex. In that order. And if my generation happened to get the order mixed up, well then, love, sex, marriage was the next best thing. I struggled to understand my mother's enthusiasm for West's desire to marry me. I had wanted my parents to help me question my decision or show a little outrage or even stop me. With deep disgust, I realized that they supported my engagement in a hopeless attempt to reinforce notions of propriety in our new era of free love, the pill, premarital sex, and all the old rules shot to hell.

★ ★ ★

At the trailer park, I met West's mother, Gladys, and his younger brother, Nelson. They were sitting outside in cheap lawn furniture in front of a double-wide. The two of them stood up when West and I made our approach. Gladys cocked her head of wiry gray hair, parted down the middle; it fanned out over her shoulders. She lifted the corner of her mouth in a half smile when West called out, "Hey, Momma!" I wondered if she was loaded. After the two brothers embraced, the four of us stood awkwardly apart.

West introduced me as his girlfriend from Massatoosey; Nelson immediately offered us his spot on the mildewed sofa, probably a throwaway found on a sidewalk. The younger brother was gangly and unhealthy looking, unashamed of his beer belly and body odor. I had to look away when his butt crack edged up above his belt line as he swept potato chip crumbs off the sofa cushions. The faded sofa gave way on squashy springs as West and I took our seats, side by side. West leaned forward, elbows on his knees, and delivered the news, "She's pregnant. And we're going to get married," he announced proudly, throwing back his shoulders.

"Sure you are. That's what your daddy said, but he never married me. Huh!" Gladys sat down with a grunt on her chaise lounge of dirty woven plastic. "Maybe this time, you can keep your ass out of jail."

"This time?" I snapped my head around and zeroed in on West.

"Oh he didn't tell you?" Gladys leaned forward over her mushrooming pot belly. "He knocked up his girlfriend in high school, and when she couldn't get him to agree to a shotgun wedding, she took a fit and smacked him with a rape charge, being underage and all. Your *boy*friend there knows *all* about how that works."

"It wasn't me, I wasn't the father, I'm telling you ..." West shook his head and looked skyward in exasperation.

"Oh sure."

"It couldn't have been me. I'm sterile," admitted West. "They made me take some tests to prove it. You wouldn't know about that." He continued giving his mother his inscrutable cat-like gaze. "You weren't exactly conscious at the time."

West's mother ignored the jab. "Oh so that's how you beat the rap? By letting God and everybody know you shoot blanks?" His mother shrugged her shoulders and snuffled as she laughed to herself with her mouth closed. "Lord Almighty, now I've heard everything."

I spoke up for the first time from my corner of the sofa. "Looks like you're not sterile anymore, West," I said, hostility rising. He ignored my acid tone, placed a hand on my knee, and gave me a broad smile. "I know! It's wonderful! All this time, I've been thinking I could never have a child, and it wasn't true! Now I'm going to have one! It's a miracle." He reached over, put his arm around me, and gave my waist a squeeze.

"What kind of doctor makes a mistake like that?" I hissed under my breath into West's ear.

"Hey, little missy. How's about speaking up for all of us to hear?" West's mother jutted her chin out. She lay there on a battered chaise lounge with broken webbing, hands folded across several rolls of midriff bulge on full view through her stained Lycra tank top.

I turned my head in her direction, struggling to maintain a semblance of courtesy, "I'm just surprised at the diagnosis, that's all."

"Yeah! No kidding! Way to go, brother," Nelson chortled. "You sure got it done!"

A wave of anger, mixed with bile, surged up from my entrails. I felt that my pregnant condition was on exhibit for all to comment on and gawk at, like a freak in a sideshow. I had completely lost control of who I was.

West got up from the sofa and held out a hand to me, pulling me up beside him. I was quick to follow his cue, grateful to leave. In his easy way, he leaned over and pulled two tickets out of his back pocket and then smiled winningly at Gladys and Nelson.

"You two got to see the show. I do the elephant act at the very end. You're going to like it. The last show is always the best."

His mother pushed her body out of her chaise lounge with difficulty and waddled over to her son, struggling to keep her balance. She plucked the two tickets out of West's hand and stuffed them into her bra right in front of us.

"What?" she had caught the look of surprise on my face, and she gave me a filthy look right in the eye. "You young females don't even bother to wear proper underwear, so—"

"Come on, Momma, just try to act right for once," growled West. Gladys didn't say another word. She looked at the two of us with a snide look of appraisal, and her head bobbed up and down slightly. Then, with a sarcastic smile on her face, she turned away. West and his mother did not appear to engage in any of the ceremonial good-byes I was used to in my family. *It had been two years since she'd seen her son*, I thought, *and this was the homecoming she gave him.*

West's mother gave us her rounded, freckled back and started shuffling over to her trailer in baggy shorts and terry slippers. At the doorstep leading up to her trailer, she paused to wipe her feet on the bedraggled shred of a faded doormat with the words *Merry Christmas* in tatters. Her large, lumpen shape disappeared behind a rusted out aluminum door as we made ready for our departure from the trailer park.

West's younger brother, Nelson, was already making his way to his beat-up hatchback. I hustled after him as he held the car door open for me, and I crawled into the sweltering chaos of the back seat. The sweet deathlike stench of leftover pot smoke, stale beer, and pizza clouded the air back there, and I tried to open the pop-out rear window to stave off a wave of nausea.

In the car, his brother was itching to ask West about Snakeboots. "How you figure you can hang out in the open in Deland? Don't you know that asshole is out looking for you?"

"He's not going to be looking for me any longer," said West

from the passenger's seat, without looking at Nelson. I saw that he faced forward, motionless, eyes on the road ahead, the solid copilot.

"How's that?" asked Nelson as he let out a puff of air between his lips. "That motherfucker has a hard-on to get back at you for screwing up that drop."

"What was I supposed to do? I thought he was dead at the wheel when the car flipped over. He lured us, Nelson. He got us all high and mighty on get-rich-quick schemes. He made us dream big dreams that were just a big load of nothing when we were young and stupid."

"Hey, speak for yourself, asshole," Nelson muttered. "I'm not the one he chose as his partner. That was you, brother."

"Yeah, well, I'll thank you not to swear in front of my lady here."

"Sorry," Nelson said quickly glancing up at me in the rearview mirror.

"Snakeboots is dead," I said flatly from the back seat, "if that's what you're worried about."

"Holy shit! You smoked him? Man!" Nelson gripped the wheel and turned to look at his brother, open-mouthed. "You're kidding me, right?"

West and I were quiet. After a pause, West said, "I didn't kill him, no. But he won't be back."

"Oh come on, man! Don't keep me in suspense!"

"Hey, there's nothing more to say," West replied testily. "We've got a baby to bring into the world. New life. New plans."

"Hoo-whee," Nelson broke out into a chuckle. "Who would have thought? My brother the fugitive: a married man—and with a child on the way. Oh man ..." He shook his head and smiled.

The car pulled up in the gravel at the edge of the lot. West hopped out of the front seat quickly and turned around to move the front seat forward so that I could extricate myself from the trash, girlie magazines, and open beer cans in the back seat. Once outside, I stood with my arms folded and waited for West to finish talking to his brother through the driver's side window.

West leaned in with one arm resting against the roof of the car and spoke to Nelson in low tones for a few minutes. As the conversation ended, the circus boy straightened up and began to back away from the car, still facing his brother.

I heard West ask, "So what did you do with my truck?"

"I traded it for this piece of crap before the repo guys came. You think I could make the payments on that thing?" Nelson looked up at his brother, squinting awkwardly in the sunlight.

"All right. Forget it. Come on down to winter quarters tomorrow," West offered.

"Better make it worth the gas. What's in it for me?"

"I'll introduce you to Superman," West said, backing away.

"Oh yeah? Is he the Man of Steel?" Nelson asked, lowering his voice.

Then, with his back still turned to me, West leaned over toward Nelson and whispered something I couldn't hear—a silly joke about kryptonite. The brothers chuckled, relaxing their necks and shoulders in a similar way. I could tell they had spent a lot of time together as children. It bothered me to hear West and Nelson talking about comic books and acting like a couple of juveniles. Three years older than me, West had always seemed so adult in my eyes.

"How about Miss Lois Lane there. Is she coming too?" Nelson looked doubtful.

"Yeah, sure," the circus boy stuffed his hands in his pockets and smiled.

"I don't know; she's seems pretty high class to me. Don't get burned, brother," Nelson replied. I wondered if he had said it just loud enough for me to hear.

West gave a shout of forced laughter and took another step back, calling out cheerfully, "Come to the show! See what you think then!" He looped an arm over my shoulder and waved to his brother with his free hand. "Thanks for the ride," he shouted out to him.

I looked Nelson in the eyes as I waved at him too, completing the image that must have looked to West's brother like a picture postcard of a happy couple on their honeymoon—waving away—smiles plastered on their faces. It dawned on me that we had become circus folk for real. Weren't we always throwing our smiles out to the audience and waving back at them from our exotic, unknowable circus world, as if to say, "Don't you wish you were here?"

I fell silent on the way back to the midway. Recorded circus music was blaring out over our scratchy loud speaker system to bring out the local populace. The smell of Blacky's greasy hamburgers floated in the air. West ambled along, unhurried. Eventually he angled his head toward me and looked into my eyes, "I know what you're thinking, Sarah," he said.

"How do *you* know?" I frowned.

"I saw how you looked at my family. You're all horrified now. You think I'm nothing but trailer trash."

I quickened my pace and fell out of step with him, eager to dodge the topic. "Your mother doesn't even like me."

"Well, you don't have to like her either," said West, placing a hand on my arm as I moved ahead of him. "You got to understand. I have no family. They're just the sorry people who brought me into this world. I'm on my own, making my own name, and I want to make my own family, the right way."

"What about that girl you got pregnant? What was that all about?" I asked tersely.

"She was trying to get me to marry her, that's all. She probably got pregnant by some other guy. I was never into her, but she wanted to have her way, and so she tried the oldest trick in the book."

"Why would any girl do *that?* It's so old-fashioned. It sounds like something out of the past when women had nothing but marriage to give them a place in the world."

"Yeah, well, it does intrigue me that you're such a hard-ass. Why won't you just say yes to me like you did the first time we made it? You were pretty sure then, and if I recall, I asked you twice if you were ready to love me. Can't you just say yes to me one more time? The last time, so we can have a life together?"

I had to give West credit. He was the opposite of the recalcitrant and moody intellectual types I had fallen for back in New England. I never had to lie in wait to see a flicker of emotion or drag his true feelings out of him with questions that frustrated both of us. He came at me head on like a locomotive—with an open heart, on fire. In love, he was fearless. I slowed my gait to fall back into step with him. We came together so easily, walking along shoulder to shoulder, the warm skin of our arms brushing now and then.

"Maybe when I said yes to you that first time, I wasn't really ready for love," I said. "I just thought I was. You can't think I could make a snap decision that would affect the rest of my life after just one night."

"Why not? I did."

"Yeah, but we didn't really know much about each other, right? I've just begun to know about your past and now your family. I'm trying to catch up." I felt as if I might be about to cry. Tears surged up, tightening my throat, "And I'm pregnant to boot!"

"And barefoot!" West prodded me in the ribs. I giggled and fell into the carefree trance of our strange and wonderful understanding. I felt as though I could fall in and out of love with West several times in one day. "What is the matter with me?" I asked him, leaning my head on his shoulder as we neared the entrance banners.

"You're pregnant." He kissed the top of my head. "And you are as beautiful as they come." Then he cupped my shoulder and gave it a little shake, adding, "And as feisty as a tigress."

"Good thing you know how to deal with the big cats then." I smiled at last.

West stopped walking mid-stride, took my face in both hands, and kissed me with all he had; he was showing me what was in store for me behind closed doors. Then he pulled back, grinned, and slid his fingers into mine and resumed walking. "Yeah, good thing," he said.

★ ★ ★

The air was warm and tropical outside Margarita's camper parked in the performers' row. Several of us—Margarita, Serpentina, Carla, Alana, the clowns, West, and I—got together around a campfire after the evening show. It would be our last meal together with the big top people. The following day, the circus would give its final performance in Deland, and then after the afternoon show, everyone would go their separate ways until the following spring when a new season would begin—another "First of May."

Many performers and concessionaires, myself included, planned on lining up early in the morning for our paychecks before circus-goers crowded the office ticket window. Only performers had the privilege of receiving weekly paychecks, but they handled their own room and board by living in their campers. And they never ate at the cookhouse. Most of the acrobats and aerialists would be heading out in their mobile homes right after the show folded. Performers' row would disappear. West and the roustabouts would be staying behind to tear down the tent and load it onto the spool truck. Then the crew would load poles, ring curbs, lighting and aerial equipment, and menagerie animals; they would take inventory and drive all the circus trucks back to winter quarters a few miles away. When they arrived there, the roustabouts would be paid in full, at last. I was mildly surprised when the circus boy told me he expected to receive two thousand dollars in cash; I knew he had been saving up for a while.

West and I sat side by side, gazing into the campfire while Margarita made noisy, joyful trips in and out of her camper for ingredients and cooking utensils. Serpentina came hobbling over on her taped-up foot and pulled something out of the pocket of her dressing gown and gave it to West. Then she smiled mysteriously at the two of us and backed away, joining Margarita back at the camper where a table had been set up for outdoor food preparations.

"Did Serpentina just hand you a gift?" I asked West.

The circus boy took my hand and produced an unusual piece of costume jewelry—a ring in the form of a coiled silver snake with two tiny rubies for eyes. He took my left hand in his palm and slid the snake ring on my finger.

"No engagement without a ring, right?" he smiled at me and waited for me to respond.

"Where on earth did she get this?" I asked, blood rising to my cheeks.

"One of Serpentina's many male fans gave it to her after he saw her perform in the sword box at the sideshow. Some old geezer—"

"*Un viejo verde!*" Serpentina shouted from the makeshift outdoor kitchen. "Me no hippie!" she called out, giving us her familiar hearty laugh. "You take it, Sarah. Is better for you. You and West. *Los novios.*" I looked down with delight at the snake ring coiled around my finger. Firelight reflected off the silver and lit up the ruby eyes. A circus engagement. And the dinner was in our honor too. I didn't know who to thank first, so I thanked them all: West, Serpentina, Margarita, the cast, the crew, the elephants, and the entire circus world.

Cooking smells of roasted chicken and garlic wafted among the campers as Margarita stirred broth into a thick layer of saffron yellow rice in a large round pan over the open fire. She and Serpentina had made enough Spanish paella to serve the entire circus crew. Their faces, glowing by the firelight, conjured up so many feelings. I was taking a last look over my shoulder at the world I had stepped into so willingly four months before. It was mid-October now, and I had missed my cue to enroll in college. I had longed to be with the circus, and I had become a part of their family. What was I going to do now that the show was coming to an end? I couldn't see myself going back to school, not after this.

LAST SHOW

14

eland. We'd reached our final destination on the route card, and I sensed that layers were peeling away everywhere, veils dropping one by one. We only had one afternoon show scheduled on our last day, which gave everyone time to pack up, or so I thought. Performers were meeting in small groups here and there in relaxed attitudes, discussing collaborations on new acts for the winter season in Europe. A monkey got loose and had to be coaxed down from one of the tent poles. Even the elephants were celebrating—Mary mounted Bessie from behind, and, with her tail between her legs, humped away on the smaller Indian elephant; Bessie creaked with pleasure.

The roustabouts and props men had been busy all morning in the big top, and I wondered what they were up to. Circus school and ladder practice had been canceled.

"What's going on in there?" I asked Red, who guarded the entrance to the main tent in his folding chair. He picked up one of the empty milk cartons at his feet and threatened to throw it at me.

"Come on, Red." I was really curious now.

"This is *our* day to go to the circus," Red replied, lifting his head and squinting up at me from under his baseball cap.

"What do you mean?"

"You'll see," he said enigmatically, raising his fuzzy eyebrows a couple of times.

I spent the idle hours tying more toy monkeys and little furry white dogs to my T-stick to sell in the ring. Closer to show time, I got dressed in a state of great anticipation, choosing my most outlandish and colorful Indian clothing: harem pants and a midriff-baring halter top covered in red embroidery and tiny mirrors.

I made my way past the sideshow and into the big top, along with the crowd of circus-goers. Afternoon light poured through the tent walls, giving the faces in the audience a yellow-green cast. The show was sold out; we had a straw house by four o'clock. Children were huddled in the straw spread in front of the general admission seats, pinching and jostling one another to get a better view. Picking my way past them, I breathed in the commingled smell of cut grass, sawdust, and animal sweat. I wanted to remember it.

As the bleachers filled up and the show got under way, a carnival-like atmosphere developed under the big top. The entire circus crew stood in the aisles and around each of the three rings to applaud the acts. They whistled and called out to the performers by name. I got held up in a knot of circus hands right next to Billy Gunga's act while I was trying to make my way past the front row seats at ringside with my toys on a stick.

Gunga's wife, "the beautiful flower of the Philippines, Miss Lily," was making her entrance in a glittering one-piece costume of peacock green. She bent her knees, dipped, and styled her arm to draw out more applause for "the one, the only, Billy *Gun*-gah!" Her sequins and beaded fringe sparkled in the spotlight as she walked in high heels toward her husband. In her hands she carried a large rectangular tray of twenty water-filled plastic glasses. I could see the water shimmer in the glasses as she stepped by, extending her long graceful legs and pointing her toes in the traditional circus girl walk. Each time, Billy Gunga stooped slightly while Miss Lily carefully placed a first, a second, and a third tray on his upturned palm.

Billy Gunga was in full jeweled-turban regalia, and he balanced the trays of water glasses on one hand, like a waiter. After each tray was added, he would go back to the center of the ring and hoist the tray tower over his head into the air in a one-handed, straight-arm press. The roustabouts exploded in vociferous applause.

I looked around at them, confused. I wondered why the circus crew was going so crazy over a trick we had all seen countless times. Deuce leaned over and whispered in my ear, "We filled them all. He's going to have to lift them all for real this time."

I stared at Deuce in disbelief and mouthed, "What?"

"We usually only fill the outer glasses at the edge of the tray," Deuce explained, "so the audience can see them. All the other plastic glasses only look full because Billy painted them inside to make it look that way."

Beads of perspiration were shining on Gunga's brown forehead when he pushed seven trays of glasses into the air. At each success, his face lit up with a wide smile of pure joy. Now Miss Lily was approaching him with two trays at a time. The audience emitted a collective, sympathetic groan. For the final tray, the water shivered in the plastic glasses while Billy Gunga strained to make the final press over his head. The circus hands called out to him in a frenzy, "Come on, Billy; you can do it!"

"You got it, man!"

"Gunga, go, go, go!"

Circus spectators looked around at the cheering circus hands who filled the aisles, as if surprised by their enthusiasm. One grandmother who was fishing a dollar out of her purse for a toy monkey leaned over to me and remarked, "Everyone seems so excited!"

"Yes," I turned to her and grinned. "This show is very exciting for us. It's our last one of the season."

All at once, Billy Gunga hoisted thirteen trays into the air, and the circus people erupted with wild applause and rushed to dissemble the trays to make way for the next act, patting Billy on the back. His wife was beaming.

"The incomparable, the magnificent Billy *Gun*-gah!" called the announcer as Gunga joined his wife in the ring for one final sweeping bow.

Meanwhile, across the tent in ring three, Carla and Alana were standing on giant blue exercise balls, maneuvering the balls backward and forward with their slipper-shod feet. A clown was making ready to toss them their juggling props. The twins were experts at juggling their hollowed-out bowling pins, but their clubs were nowhere to be found in the props basket. The clown looked a little quizzical and performed a frantic "I can't find your props" pantomime. He scurried all over the ring, looking everywhere, comically lifting the ringmaster's red coat tails before heading out into the crowd where he searched under the feet of three giggling children. Suddenly we heard a wolf whistle, and one of the circus hands approached the clown with a rubber chicken and a box full of grapefruit and oranges from the cookhouse.

The circus girls, balancing in anticipation on their blue balls, laughed in surprise and reached out to the clown. The hobo clown gave a Charlie Chaplin mock shrug and began tossing grapefruit and oranges to each of the juggling twins. The sisters were off, improvising a new routine on the spot, creating a spectacle of yellow and orange, juggling both individually and as a pair. All the while, they careened around the ring on their huge blue balls, varying their distance from one another. When they hopped off their exercise balls into the sawdust to close the act, two men heaved a large watermelon in their direction, which they caught together, seamlessly, all four hands lifting the watermelon into the air for their final victory stance.

"This is amazing!" I hollered to Red over the noise of the applause. He had joined our group of roustabouts by the ring. "Is this what happens at the end of the run?"

"Yeah," Red said, looking away distractedly. "They try to trick up every act. I hear they got real policemen coming to bust up the clown act when they do their Wild West saloon fight."

Across the ring, I saw West disappear through the tent flaps. The lights went down. A spotlight picked up the dazzling slender figure of Mirabella in a leopard bikini and a feathered tiara. As she prepared to wrap her sinuous body around the trapeze, her signature music came on. Soon, she was sweeping over the crowd in full flow in time with the classical music she loved. As the act transitioned to the difficult tricks performed with the trapeze at rest, the music changed without warning to the bawdy lascivious blare of trumpets belting out a tune known as "The Stripper."

Unfazed, Mirabella completed her routine and hung upside down from the bar by her heels an extra beat and then shocked everyone under the tent by releasing her feet and catapulting her body upward to grab the bar with both hands in a gravity-defying move. Then she dropped straight down into her husband's arms; he caught her slight body easily. Cradled safely in Swede's arms, with the stripper music still playing, Mirabella kicked her long legs in a saucy way and responded to a beery cat call of "take it off" by tossing her feather tiara into the crowd.

"I saw this circus in Alabama," I heard someone say, "and it was nothing like this! This is the best show I've ever seen!"

I felt the same way but for different reasons. I had seen the show every day for four months, but this performance completed my initiation into circus life. I was grateful to Red for making sure I was surprised by the last show tradition of pranking all the acts. This moment of sheer wonder and joy was the reason I left home to join the circus back in July—a lifetime ago. He must have known what it would mean to me.

I made another round up into the stands and sold toys at half price; some I let go for a quarter. What did it matter now? Whoever wanted a toy that night was going to get one. Then I positioned myself in a good spot to see the clown act, glowing in the knowledge that I was in on the prank this time.

The slapstick saloon fight began; one clown burst through a set of shuttered saloon doors, and the other began brawling with him, using sound effects to enhance their stage fight. They went after each other. The hobo clown brandished a fake gun and fired blanks at the floppy feet of his adversary. At the sound of the first pop-pop-pop of gunfire, two real uniformed police officers, armed with Colt .45s, stormed the center ring and proceeded to handcuff the two clowns. Bewildered, the performers fell out of character, wondering for an instant if they were actually going to jail, while the crowd laughed along with the pantomime, assuming it was all part of the show. Only when the four struggling men exited through the velvet curtains and the policemen relaxed and high-fived their oversized white rubber hands did the clowns realize that it had all been in fun.

"I can't believe they'd trick up the elephant act—the way them elephants been acting up lately." Red was right next to me, but he had to yell to be heard above the din of the crowd.

Bessie and Mary had been unpredictable all season, but West's elephant act was fair game. One of the roustabouts had replaced their juggling clubs with pineapples, making them impossible to use in the ring. The elephants would refuse to grip the fruit's spiny, unfamiliar texture. Then there was the unexpected casting change. An injured Serpentina had agreed to step aside, allowing thirteen-year-old Celeste Lefèvre to take her place as the female elephant rider. Celeste even got to perform a spin, balancing one foot on Bessie's trunk and extending one leg into a graceful arabesque as she gripped the elephant's head harness. The Indian elephant turned around and around before placing her young lady performer gently back on the sawdust in the center ring.

The crowd applauded loudly, hooted and stamped their feet, encouraged by the roustabout at ringside who gave wolf whistles and urged Celeste to perform the "under the belly" trick—the jewel in the crown for the final act of the final show. The diminutive teenager stood lightly in front of the elephant, reached over her head with both hands, gripped Bessie's neck harness, and then scooted herself under the elephant's belly. Bessie immediately folded her entire body forward and balanced her weight on her curled-up trunk. Celeste lay prone on the ground underneath while Bessie lifted her hindquarters in the air and balanced her knees on her elephant elbows in the tripod position. The crowd waited expectantly for Celeste to reappear, wondering if the performer had been crushed to death underneath.

The finale required the elephant girl to emerge intact on the other side of the elephant, jumping up to full extension, hands raised in triumph beneath Bessie's lifted hind legs. The trick never failed to generate a huge wave of applause. But Celeste was grandstanding and remained prone, trying to build up suspense by keeping the elephant waiting, balanced on her trunk.

Finally, the elephant had had enough; too late I noticed that Bessie had that merry look in her eye. Just as Celeste hopped up from underneath and threw her arms overhead to receive her ovation, she was doused from above with what looked like a bucket of water—typical arcade-style slapstick, it appeared. The audience gasped in surprise and then rocked with laughter, falling all over themselves. It was sheer pandemonium. In amazement, I realized that Bessie had let fly a full bladder of elephant urine in a soaking downpour all over the young performer.

Celeste ran screaming from the ring, hands held to her face, feathered tiara wet and bedraggled. West hustled the elephants out of the ring hurriedly. It was to be his last performance.

I dropped my empty T-stick and pushed past eager rubbernecking locals who crowded the exit corridor and then made my way at a run around the curve of the big top to the backyard where the performers waited to go on for the final full-cast parade. I lifted a section of tent wall and joined the others in the canvas-lined corridor where I saw Serpentina leading a sobbing

Celeste back to her family's mobile home. Deuce and Shorty had already doused the ringmaster's daughter with buckets of water.

West stood in between the large heads of both elephants, gently holding on to their head harnesses, waiting to go on for his curtain call. He was trying hard to control his mirth. When the circus boy looked at me poker-faced, I could see laughter dancing in his eyes. I had to pull my lips under my teeth and bite down not to erupt in a fit of giggles.

Calliope music began to play, cuing the entire troupe to line up in a canvas-lined corridor behind the velvet entrance curtains. The time had come for our final farewell parade around the big top. First in line, Fritz and his Eskimo dogs took off at a clip and ran out to take a bow. When the clowns went out for their curtain call, they were joined by the two local policemen who had pranked their act. I smiled generously at the officers as they made their way past me to line up with the clowns. When they nodded back at me and politely tipped their hats, I knew I was out of danger. Through the open curtains, I could see all four men—two in costume and two in uniform—taking a bow to shouts of laughter.

West guided his elephants into place at the end of the line; they would go on last. The circus boy climbed on top of Mary and beckoned to me. When I walked over, he tilted his head in Bessie's direction.

"Want a ride?" he smiled down at me from his perch on top of his lead elephant, Mary. "You look like a princess from the *Arabian Nights* in those harem pants." I put my hand on my hip, cocked my head to one side, and looked up at him, unsure. "Come on! *Someone* has got to ride Bessie," West implored. I hesitated, smiling. "Bessie loves you now. You know she does." West broke into a grin. "We all do!" he enthused, waving me forward with both hands now.

As I approached Bessie, West twisted around in his seat on Mary's back to command his second elephant. Bessie dropped her trunk to the ground and, on West's cue, curled it up slightly in the shape of a fishhook, providing me with a foothold. I placed my foot in the saddle of her trunk, and she lifted me up onto her back. The other performers were circling the ring, and our music came up. West gave us one backward glance, and I quickly straddled Bessie's neck, stroking her behind the ears and squeezing with my legs. She lumbered forward and broke into an elephant trot. As the elephants broke through the velvet curtains out into the large expanse of golden, sawdust-filled air under the big top, the roar of the crowd intensified. People jumped to their feet; their cheers came at us like a wave that swelled and burst open. We were surrounded by a rushing sound that filled the air, as if we had entered a tunnel at top speed with the windows down.

The tent was shaking with applause as the crowd whistled, called out, and stomped their feet on the boards. I was riding high up on Bessie, and, as I looked down at the audience— wearing the electric smile of a bally girl—I waved my arm over my head in a sweeping arc. Out of habit, and in time with the music, Bessie followed Mary's lead, taking a full lap around the track just outside the performance rings before heading out the main exit. We were the last act of the last performance and the last to take our bows and wave good-bye to rows and rows of rapt faces. The curtains closed behind Bessie's tail as I urged her through to the back yard, and the show was over.

Behind the scenes, circus performers were sharing a final moment of triumph: men were clapping each other on the back, and women were hugging and kissing fellow performers on both cheeks. The older Palmieri children performed exuberant cartwheels and backflips while Silvana, the youngest, picked up a show dog's front paws and started to dance. The Spitz eagerly obeyed, waltzing back and forth on hind legs. West retreated in the direction of Lefèvre's mobile home. I assumed that he needed to check on Celeste and offer an apology for his elephant's behavior.

The crowd of circus-goers was soon spilling out of the tent into the warm afternoon. The big top appeared to hover in the distance like a specter in the hazy, humid air. Waves of murmuring silhouettes could be seen ambling across the grass, making their way to their cars.

I doubled back through the sideshow entrance to take one last look inside the empty big top tent. The atmosphere inside was mysterious and silent but still alive somehow with remembered voices: "We hope you've had a pleasant afternoon. This is the final performance of the Reyes Bros. Ragtime Gypsy Show East Coast tour. We hope you'll all come back and see us again next year."

★ ★ ★

While West was at teardown, I went back to our sleeper and began to pack up my things. I pulled my tent roll out from under the bed. The canvas was coated in dust, but all the pieces were there. Under the drooping gray bedsheet, way back in the far corner, I spied the juggling pins in their white vinyl zippered case. I got on my belly and hauled it out. We would need to return the juggling pins to Carla and Alana today. I hadn't been practicing much since I'd started learning the aerial routines. I opened the case. The three clubs were nestled securely inside in form-fitting foam inserts. With tenderness, I pulled them out one by one and brought them out into the sunlight for one last go.

Down on the grass next to our truck, I laid out a blanket and set up for my routine. I threw one club in the air and watched it spin and caught it in my hand. The club seemed lighter to me than I remembered. I wondered if West had altered the weighted beads inside the club after performing in the ring with his elephants. I tried a basic warmup, a simple throw/catch with two pins. But when I attempted to add in the third for the circular juggle, the clubs flew away at odd angles and landed unceremoniously in the dirt. One of them even came loose at the neck.

After collecting all three clubs, I sat down on my blanket cross-legged and proceeded to unscrew the top of the damaged pin. A sinking feeling crept into my abdomen as the top of the club came away in my hand: the neck was stuffed with a wad of cotton like a bottle of aspirin. I pulled out the cotton with two fingers and looked inside. The hollowed-out belly of the juggling pin held multiple plastic packets of refined white and blue powders and a large cache of pills.

I glanced around, my thoughts accelerating even as my movements remained calm and deliberate. West and the crew were still tearing down the big top tent and loading the pole truck to take the circus equipment back to winter quarters. There weren't any other circus people about; most of the performers had already left in their mobile homes. I screwed the top back on the club in a swift movement and zipped up the case. Then I set the case aside and performed a couple of backbends, stretching out with my hands to the sky one last time before I lazily shook out and folded up the blanket for the benefit of anyone who might be watching me from a distance. I had learned from West how to mask any signs of panic by displaying an unhurried attitude. Inside, I was overwhelmed by the urge to flee. Adrenaline was shrieking through my veins; I could feel the tingling rush shooting down my arms and legs to my extremities.

I threw the blanket into the truck cab and bounded up into our sleeper with the vinyl case strapped over my shoulder. I remained on all fours on the wooden floor with the case in front of me. I knelt back on my heels and yanked the snake ring off my finger and slipped it into the case. Then I pushed the case—clubs, drugs, and all—back under the bed, next to my dusty tent roll. I stood up, took one last sweeping look at the place that had been my home, grabbed my army duffel off the bed, and left my tent roll behind. I slipped unseen down to the truck engine; I squatted there for an instant to get a read on the activity on the lot. No one was coming. I saw a hawk up in the sky, winging its way over an open field, and I was gone.

★ ★ ★

In 1971, before Roe v. Wade, abortions were illegal in many states including Massachusetts and New Hampshire, and the only way for me to get one was to head for New York through an organized underground of female medical services. A girlfriend, who had enrolled at Columbia University, tracked down a hospital and a doctor through a hotline. I would have to rush north without wasting a day because I was in my ninth week of pregnancy. Head down, I ran for it. I got on a bus and then a plane and left the circus world forever.

Twenty-four hours after touching down at LaGuardia, I was going up a flight of stairs with a dozen other young women of all races; we were herded in front of a row of tables displaying an array of contraceptive devices. We could select our birth control method of choice at no cost. At the time, I wanted to use everything at once, having lost faith in the reliability of condoms and diaphragms on their own. I had already tried the pill, which made me vomit, so I opted for an IUD known as the Dalkon Shield, said to be very effective. The doctor would insert it for free after performing the "D and C." I was never told what those letters stood for.

The nurse explained that I was to remain as still as possible on the examination table; if I moved even slightly, the doctor risked perforating my uterus, and I wouldn't be able to have children in the future. To help us understand what was happening to us, all the female patients received a free copy of an informational pamphlet printed on cheap newsprint entitled *Our Bodies, Ourselves*. I never threw it away.

It took me no time to make friends with the black girl in line next to me named Sheila. We swapped stories about our boyfriends who had gotten us pregnant, how we were no longer with them, and how we had come up with the abortion money on our own. All my savings from the circus bought me a plane ʼ and the abortion fee.

After our procedures, we met up again in an outpatient waiting room where they gave us a survey to fill out. At one point, as we sifted through the multiple-choice questionnaire, Sheila let out a snort, "How do I feel now?"

I had been eyeing the choices for question number nineteen and was hovering over the bubble next to "depressed."

"Relieved! That's how I feel!" Sheila erupted. "No more leaning over the toilet every morning. No more arguing with my boyfriend. No more freaking out about money. Re-*lieved!*" Sheila bent over to scratch in her answer.

I thought about how I had never said good-bye to West, but I knew he would eventually look under the bed for the vinyl case and find the serpent ring nestled in with the stash of drugs for his next big drop. Then he might guess why I hadn't returned to his side this time.

I imagined the circus boy introducing his no-account brother, Nelson, to "Superman," his money man, the "Man of Steel" at winter quarters. It wasn't until I had boarded the plane to New York and faced a long stretch of empty hours in the air that it dawned on me I had known who "Superman" was all along: Wayne, the water boy.

I had my own theories as to how West had come into such a large quantity of hard drugs at the end of the tour, but I tried to push those thoughts from my mind—pretend that it had never happened and that I hadn't really seen anything. I did suspect that Snakeboots had robbed and murdered Jesse for the double shipment that went missing. And maybe West had pilfered the stolen drugs off an unconscious Snakeboots and kept them for himself while I'd gone running to find the ringmaster. *For all I knew,* I thought—which was nothing and would remain so.

I had no doubt that "Superman" and West were still doing business together. I pictured them making the two-thousand-dollar deal in a hangar at winter quarters. Wayne could come out of the shadows, now that the performers were gone. I wondered if West and Wayne—two outcasts for different reasons—would harden into outlaws or if West had secretly planned to make one last lucrative drop once we reached winter quarters so that he could leave the country and start over. I would never know.

EPILOGUE

On a summer day in July the following year, I found myself on a train from Boston to Old Saybrook, Connecticut, once again looking to meet up with the Reyes Bros. Ragtime Gypsy Show. The reunion was bittersweet. Margarita, Billy Gunga, and the clowns recognized me in an instant and ushered me over to their mobile homes. While I sat outside Billy Gunga's trailer, catching up with Lily, the juggling twins, and Margarita, someone—a man—came up to me from behind and placed his hands over my eyes without a word. I was terrified and embarrassed. What if it was who I hoped it was? What if I guessed wrong?

Everyone waited, enjoying the spectacle. I turned and recognized Fritz, the hobo clown, who smiled whimsically at me and doffed his hat; then he leaned over and squirted me in the face with the flower on his lapel.

I heard a familiar cackle. Red Maynard was making his way over, limping badly with a noticeable hitch in his stride. He paused to balance himself in place, and, with an outstretched arm, he broke into song, "Can I sleep in your barn tonight? I have no tobacco and no matches. I'll be gone in the mornin'…"

"Where you been, you old circus bum?" I laughed, running

over to meet him half way. Recorded calliope music floated over the air; the afternoon show was about to begin, and I wanted to talk to Red alone.

I waved back to everyone gathered outside Billy's camper and called over, "See you at the show!" I took Red's scaly arm to help walk him back to his truck.

I learned all I needed to know. West was hiding out in the swamp, running from the law again. He had come to the lot once, late at night, to say good-bye to Red, but the old man couldn't convince him to join up with the circus again. "Said he didn't want to have anything to do with circus girls for a good while," declared Red, shaking his head.

I'd written West a harsh letter after Halloween the previous fall and mailed it to winter quarters, c/o Reyes Bros. Ragtime Gypsy Show. I let him know that I'd had an illegal abortion, performed by a black doctor, who was kind and serious, attended by a white nurse who let me squeeze her hand and look at her face—her dark eyes locked on mine—until the atrocious minutes had passed. I described how much it hurt without anesthesia, "like getting your dick caught in the zipper of your monkey suit." I didn't tell him I was also full of a deep remorse, a sadness that blew my spirit clear out of my body, like a chill wind through an empty house. No one had told me about the sadness that would follow me for months, then years. I felt as if I had lost a life. And I had.

But I couldn't find a way to describe my confusion over never finding my circus again. It had changed in my eyes. A new trainer had taken over as elephant handler, and he treated Bessie and Mary badly—even used the bull hook on their ears, right in the ring. I felt sorry for Rudy; Margarita didn't really love him any-more, and she flirted with all the new circus hands. I saw every-thing for what it was. I did glimpse a few bright, colorful flashes, but I felt no yearning to join up with the show again. The air was sticky sweet by the pie car; litter drifted in the grass.

"It's falling apart more and more every year," Red mused as he rested against the hood of his truck. "The price of gas is going to put us out of business."

I could smell the diesel oil from the trucks mixed with cut grass.

We had been right, my artistic friends and I, back in high school when we were salvaging pieces of Americana. In Boston, cranes were sprouting up all over the city, knocking down funky old sections of the South End, block by block.

In the summer of 1971, something was dying in America right in front of us. I had witnessed one of the final years of a traveling circus, the last of the Sunday afternoons when roustabouts would gather under the shadow of a painted circus truck, sit on bales of hay or on blankets in the grass, and listen to Red spin his circus stories. He'd describe how he had stolen horses in the night for a show by painting their bellies with silver to give them the appearance of a different breed; how one night, when the tent canvas caught fire, he and the circus crew threw everything into the river, even the bleachers; how Celeste's best friend lost her life when she fell to her death from the Spanish web because the circus had to set up in a goddamn parking lot, and the blood streamed from her eyes.

"That's all you have in the end, and, believe me, I know." Red looked at me with filmy eyes. "You're not going to see me here next year."

"What do you mean, Red?" I asked, knowing that this visit to the Reyes Bros. circus would be my last.

"Our stories. That's all we have to give after a life in the circus." Red reached his hand out to me and held it. "And, Miss Sarah, you have a story to tell. One hell of a story."

★ ★ ★

People still ask me if it's true: did you really run away with the circus? To the outsider, I guess I did run. But to me, I didn't run away so much as fly straight into the bright, fiery light that was the Reyes Bros. Ragtime Gypsy Show—four months of high brilliance during my moth years—when the flame was all I could see.

ACKNOWLEDGMENTS

This book would not have been possible without the uncommon understanding of my parents, Ruth and Steve who allowed me to join a traveling circus as a teenager in 1971. I am indebted to two people for bringing my circus story out into the light after forty-five years in hiding—Tito W. James and Romana Lowe, whose unflagging support, encouragement and advice sustained me throughout the process of creating a fictional world out of a handful of anecdotes, memories and photographs. Sincerest thanks also to Jessica Moreland and Katherine Wellington who helped me with my earliest drafts, and to Gwen Ash and the entire team at Archway Publishing from Simon and Schuster for making the book a reality.

I am deeply grateful to the following organizations for helping to bring this project to fruition by providing opportunities for writers to do research and hone their craft: Grub Street of Boston, Tucson Festival of Books, and The Circus Historical Society.

Finally, I wish to thank the circus people I have known for their gift of friendship. You are fondly remembered.

CPSIA information can be obtained
at www.ICGtesting.com
Printed in the USA
LVOW08s1639240117
522002LV00003B/552/P

9 781480 834705